T0082556

BRIDGET CANTWELL

authorHOUSE®

AuthorHouse™
1663 Liberty Drive
Bloomington, IN 47403
www.authorhouse.com
Phone: 1 (800) 839-8640

Published by AuthorHouse 01/09/2018

ISBN: 978-1-5462-2384-9 (sc)
ISBN: 978-1-5462-2385-6 (e)

Print information available on the last page.

This book is printed on acid-free paper.

Chapter One

Gabriella stood beside her father's grave long after everyone else had departed. The small cemetery lay beside an old chapel on a steep hillside above a lake. Gabriella did not look at the view across the lake to the wooded foothills beyond, or to the mountains in the distance, or even to a glimpse of the ocean far away down the valley. She appeared rooted in her grief.

As the light faded in the late afternoon, the chill brought Gabriella to a sense of her surroundings. She reluctantly raised her head to look at the setting sun, laid a rose on the damp earth and turned towards home.

By the time Gabriella entered the house by the back kitchen door it was dark. The old housekeeper, who was about to lift a tea tray, forgot it, turned to her young mistress and folded her in her arms.

'Where have you been, child?' she asked. 'If I had not been so busy with the guests above I would have come to look for you.'

'I did not realise the time, Nanny. I'm sorry to have worried you.'

'It's understandable. Now sit by the fire while I take this tea tray upstairs. Most people have left now. All of them asked for you. There's tea in my old teapot for you. You'll be needing it. I won't be long.'

* * *

Upstairs the housekeeper placed the tray before Gabriella's

step-mother who graciously poured tea for the few remaining guests who were awkwardly attempting to sympathise.

'Yes,' said Mrs. Valencie, 'it has been a most difficult time for me. It has been such a shock. My dear husband appeared to be in such good health. I did, of course, do everything in my power to find some sort of cure, but it was all hopeless.' She dabbed her eyes gently with a handkerchief.

'But,' she continued, 'the doctors all said that in the case of severe stroke there is so little one can do, except to alleviate the symptoms as much as possible. I'm sure I did everything I could to make my dear husband's last few days as comfortable as possible.'

The guests murmured their agreement and drank their tea.

'Well, I must be of good courage now and overcome my grief as best I can. I have three daughters to think about and take care of now without any support. I expect there will be much for me to do in the next few weeks, what with legal matters and so on. Gabriella can be a little difficult at times but I will do my best for her. I am sure Matilda and Florence will do all they can to help.'

An elderly gentleman rose from his seat and stated that although he was reluctant to leave dear Mrs. Valencie, he thought that she must want a little time to herself. 'The King and Queen send their condolences, of course. A lady-in-waiting will call tomorrow to see how things stand with you, if that is convenient.'

Mrs. Valencie said she would be honoured to receive the lady.

The old butler fetched coats and hats for the King's Secretary and the other guests as they assembled in the hall and, after Mrs. Valencie had said her goodbyes, watched them safely down the steps to their waiting carriages.

'Well, girls,' said Mrs. Valencie, as she and two of her daughters arranged themselves before the fire. 'I think that went very well. The Secretary might do something for us, it seems. Maybe you will get invitations to the Palace occasionally. If so, we must do everything we can to take advantage of any opportunities that come our way.'

Matilda and Florence, both florid young ladies, looked pleased, although not too sure what the opportunities could result in.

Mrs. Valencie's pleasant thoughts were interrupted as she remembered her step-daughter. 'Wherever is Gabriella? I am most displeased she was not present to help with our guests. But she will always do whatever suits her best, so I suppose it is no surprise.'

The evening passed slowly. The butler, who was the housekeeper's husband, announced dinner. The dining room was a little chilly because the fire had not been alight for very long. Mrs. Valencie asked the butler to make sure that Gabriella came to the table if he could find her.

The butler, Mr. Georges, knew where she was but wished Mrs. Valencie would excuse Miss Gabriella this day of all days. He knew it was pointless to suggest that Gabriella have a small meal in the kitchen with Nanny.

So the four ladies ate their soup. Matilda complained about being cold. Florence said she did not like the soup. Mrs. Valencie grumbled that the fire was not hot enough, that the soup was lukewarm, that the main course of lamb stew was very frugal and had not been cooked well. She stated she would speak to the housekeeper tomorrow. Even though the master of the house was no longer with them, Mrs. Valencie opined, they still had to keep up standards.

Gabriella had swallowed a few mouthfuls of soup but could not manage anything else. She waited silently until the meal finished when she could retire to her room. She fell asleep from exhaustion after hours of weeping into her pillow.

Early the next morning Mrs. Valencie, knowing she could not expect the lady-in-waiting until after lunch, set out to visit her husband's solicitor.

Chapter Two

The small kingdom of Essenia is squeezed between two larger and more powerful countries, Grelland to the north and Farren to the south. Fortunately neither country ever had invaded Essenia, mostly because it held no strategic or economic benefits, and because each of the powerful countries preferred to have Essenia on its border than the alternative. Therefore Essenia was a peaceful place to live. But it was not the most affluent.

The King and Queen of Essenia had more responsibilities than they could comfortably cope with, given the amount of money to hand. The previous year had seen devastating floods in the valleys of this mountainous country and the King had felt obliged to help rebuild damaged houses and give what relief he could where harvests had failed. The income from taxes did not cover the expense, nor did they even cover the expenses of the Palace, and the King was obliged to make up the difference from his own fortune. Fortune is probably the wrong word and the difficulties left the King with little resources.

The grandly named Palace was, in fact, simply a large house. However, it was situated in beautiful surroundings and had extensive gardens. Sitting on a rise of ground beside a lake, the Palace had views across it to the mountains beyond.

The King's servants were all getting older and some should have retired long ago. The staffing levels, which had never been high, had dropped even more since the disaster of last year and each of the staff now had to do more than one job. Employing younger and more energetic staff could not be thought of while the funds were so low. Matters were brought to a head when the cook, now seventy five years of age, reluctantly said she felt she would need some more help in the kitchen. The King knew she should retire and therefore insisted that she accept a small pension and go to live with her slightly younger sister on a nearby farm. This, of course, left a vacancy in the palace staff.

The King discussed the problem with the Queen and his Secretary.

'I am wondering what is best to do,' he stated. 'Have you been able to find anyone who would be suitable, Mr. Secretary?'

'Well, Sir,' said the Secretary, 'I have made some enquiries. There are several suitable candidates. The problem is that most of them think your funds are unlimited and want to cook very expensive dishes every day. They all want extremely large salaries too. The Palace finances could not cope with such expenditure because it would mean we would not be able to do anything else. We still need to entertain a little and if, in future, we had need of, say, a butler, we would not be in a position to afford one. I considered taking on a young person but the thought of working in the royal kitchens appears to overwhelm the ones I spoke to. I am at a loss to know what to suggest.'

They pondered the problem for a while until the Queen said she would make a cup of tea for them all. She went down to the kitchen, with which she was familiar. She had spent many a cold afternoon with the cook, enjoying the warmth of the ovens, while the cook pottered with her cakes. The Palace was not noted for its formalities.

Upon her return, the Queen found her husband and his

secretary slightly despondent. 'What are we going to do about dinner when the cook leaves?' asked the King.

The Queen smiled. 'I have an announcement to make,' she said. 'I am going to do the cooking myself. I am tired of watercolours and needlework, and neighbours have so little time to visit these days that I find myself unoccupied for much of the time. I have helped our cook from time to time and have watched what she does, so it will not be a problem at all. The scullery maid can help. She does all the marketing anyway. Yes, I will cope with it very well and will enjoy doing it at the same time.'

The Queen waved away all the objections from her kind husband and said she would organise matters that very day.

'And, by the way, Mr. Secretary, seeing that I do not have a lady-in-waiting, who did you send to visit Mrs. Valencie?' asked the Queen.

'Ah yes,' said the Secretary. 'Our good neighbour, Mrs. Rodriguez, went.'

Mrs. Rodriguez lived in a large house in the small town near the Palace. She was a widow with a comfortable income who had little to do, so she enjoyed taking part in the Palace's affairs if they did not require much exertion.

'Mrs. Rodriguez said she would find it interesting to see what sort of set up Mrs. Valencie was running. She told me afterwards that she had spent an exhausting afternoon listening to Mrs. Valencie's troubles, but she felt sorry for her two daughters, who do not appear to have many natural advantages.'

'A bit plain, are they?' asked the Queen.

'I'm not very well versed in these matters but I would say that plain is a good word to use. Miss Gabriella puts them in the shade. Of course, Miss Gabriella puts most young ladies in the shade. Mrs. Rodriguez said she ventured to hint that an invitation to the Palace on open days might be forthcoming. Unfortunately neither I nor Mrs. Rodriguez were able to have a word with Miss Gabriella, so we do not know yet what her situation is. But I expect she will attend the open days with her step-sisters.'

* * *

Mrs. Valencie had found the solicitor's office in the main street of the village nearest to the Palace. As she entered a little bell rang above the door. A clerk seated at a small desk raised his head from his writing and greeted her. He invited her to sit by the fire while he went to inform the solicitor she had arrived.

She was kept waiting while the clerk bustled about locating several bundles of documents for the solicitor. Mrs. Valencie tried to maintain an appearance of outer calm but after ten minutes she interrupted the clerk's work by telling him that he was to inform the solicitor that she had an important document to show him, before the solicitor went any further with his work on her behalf. The clerk told her he would do so but kept her waiting for another five minutes.

Upon being invited to enter the solicitor's office, Mrs. Valencie did so with an ill-concealed impatience. She strode into a warm office and sat in a chair before a large desk covered in papers. The solicitor, a portly older man, stood and offered his hand which Mrs. Valencie shook briefly.

'My husband's new will,' stated Mrs. Valencie without any preliminaries. She handed a document to the solicitor. 'When my dear husband realised he would probably pass away,' Mrs Valencie dabbed her eyes delicately with her handkerchief, 'he realised his affairs would be better cared for by me than by his young, inexperienced daughter. He has changed his will accordingly. Unfortunately he then became too ill to bring it to you himself, but you will find it in order.'

Mr. Browning, the solicitor, took the papers and said he would read them carefully if Mrs. Valencie would excuse his being quiet for a moment. Silence descended on the office. Mrs. Valencie shuffled about on her chair.

'Well now,' said Mr. Browning at length. 'This seems to be in order.'

Mrs. Valencie breathed out and relaxed a little. 'Of course,' she said.

'The wording is not what I would have chosen but the intent appears to be clear. I note your two daughters were witnesses. So now to the particulars: It seem you are to be the sole beneficiary of Mr. Valencie's property to do with as you deem fit and right in whatever circumstances you find yourself and in the sincere belief you will administer the property to the best of your ability and will provide for your daughters.

'At this point,' continued the solicitor, 'if Mr. Valencie had been able to apprise me of his intentions I would have advised him to name you particularly instead of simply writing 'his dear wife'. Also I would have advised Mr. Valencie to name the daughters so there can be no doubt as to his meaning. Obviously, he meant all three of your daughters but this matter must be clarified before we can proceed.'

'I see no need to do that whatsoever, Mr. Browning. My husband trusted me to look after the girls and I will do so naturally.'

'Yes, naturally, but consider this. It is my duty to advise you properly and, if in future Miss Gabriella had any reason to contest this clause, she would undoubtedly succeed. Likely she would go to one of the solicitors in the city, who would not only contest that clause but the complete will. Should that happen this will may be disregarded and the old one reinstated. As you know this would place Miss Gabriella as the main beneficiary, with you and your daughters dependent on her good will.'

Mrs. Valencie paled. 'That cannot happen surely.'

'I am simply informing you of the possibilities. I have to consider all eventualities however remote they may be.'

'So what do I do?'

'I will direct my clerk to prepare a document clarifying who the daughters are as mentioned in the will and then we can proceed to finalise the will. This will take some time but it is a very important matter.'

'Very well, if we must,' Mrs. Valencie paused. 'How much money will there be?'

'I have the details to hand.' Mr. Browning handed Mrs. Valencie a sheet of paper with various amounts carefully written upon it. 'Perhaps I had better explain it.'

Mr. Browning showed her the principle amount of money which was invested in various ways. Below it were the small amounts of interest accruing from each of the investments. 'You will end up with about five hundred sovereigns a year.'

'Is that all?' cried Mrs. Valencie. 'Where has all the money gone? There was surely much more than this.'

'Mr. Valencie's business has suffered some losses recently for reasons unknown. It is always unfortunate when these things happen but we have to cope with circumstances as we find them. Five hundred sovereigns is a nice sum and you should manage quite well with a little economy.'

'But I have one or two outstanding bills I must pay. My husband neglected his responsibilities and has left me in this dreadful situation. I will have to have some of the money which is invested in order to put matters right.'

'Unfortunately that will not be possible,' said Mr. Browning calmly. 'A will takes a long time to be put into action and I must take the proper steps to do all the necessary legal work before you can avail of the principle. I will advance you some of the interest so that you will have something to live on. In fact, I must strenuously advise you not to use the principle or you will find your income severely curtailed in later years.'

'But what am I to do with the bills?' Mrs Valencie wailed.

'Send them to me and I will undertake to pay them off gradually. Creditors will occasionally forgo pressing for payment if they can rely on the money coming eventually.'

'I will see to them myself,' said Mrs. Valencie grumpily.

'Very well,' said the solicitor and he stood to show Mrs. Valencie to the door.

Chapter Three

The King and Queen of Essenia were now middle aged and had long given up expecting an heir. Therefore from time to time the problem of the succession had arisen and the King had recently asked his Secretary to discover the closest relative who could possibly be thought to be suitable as heir to the throne.

'Given that the heir will not inherit such a great deal,' said the King, 'we might find someone who is from a reasonably humble background, while still being of good parentage.'

The Secretary said he would give the matter priority. He studied the archives and took legal advice from the King's solicitor and over time a candidate became apparent.

Not far from the Palace lived a merchant who had descended from a brother of the King's grandfather. He had not made a huge success of his business but it provided a comfortable income for himself and his young nephew. This young person, named James, had lost his parents at an early age but had been so kindly received by his uncle that he did not suffer as some others might have done. His childhood had been happy. James had spent idyllic summers playing with two of his friends and neighbours, Peter Eston and Gabriella Valencie. They had frolicked in the gardens or splashed about on the lake with makeshift rafts. Sometimes they had trekked in the woods, taking along a dog and a pony to carry the sandwiches.

Gabriella, Peter and James had been inseparable. There had been a quiet time when Gabriella's mother had died. At that difficult time, James and Peter did not know how to help Gabriella and had tiptoed around her, being extraordinarily kind. But the housekeeper, who was also the nanny, soon sent the young girl out to play to help her recover. So the years passed. As the children grew older, their lessons took up more time and circumstances limited their time together. James was to spend more time learning his uncle's business. Peter was taken on by James's uncle as an apprentice. Life was to part the three for a short time.

The King's Secretary was able to give the King two names which he felt might suit as heirs to the throne. Both young men were as near to the King in relationship as was possible. One of them was James and the other was a young man who lived in the neighbouring country of Grelland. This young nobleman named Roland had been brought up in the Grelland Court and was used to a very different life than he would be able to have in Essenia. Therefore it was felt that James would be the best candidate. Besides which, James had descended from a favourite aunt of the King, whereas the other young man's mother had been the daughter of a younger aunt who apparently had been known as something of a tyrant.

The Secretary wrote to Roland and explained the situation, hoping Roland would be happy to allow his kinsman to take on the duties of the King of Essenia. Roland, knowing that Essenia would not enrich but rather be a drain on his resources, readily wrote back to say he was pleased for his distant kinsman to have the privilege of being heir to the throne.

The King asked James's uncle to visit the Palace so that the King could explain the situation and ask his permission that James should live at the palace. The merchant was saddened to think he would lose James, but soon realised that it was in James's best interests to live at the palace and learn his new duties. The merchant knew he would not see so much of James but at least he was not far away. The Queen had issued an open invitation for the merchant to dine with them often.

James was not so sure about the change to his life. At eighteen years of age he had thought he would follow in his uncle's footsteps. It was not too easy to change his whole outlook. Being King would bring huge responsibility but very little in the way of income. However, James had been brought up with a sense of duty which, in the end, won out and James went to live with the King and Queen.

Chapter Four

Four days after Mrs. Valencie returned from her trip to the solicitor, she called Gabriella to her sitting room.

'Sit down, Gabriella, and please listen to me carefully. I would be grateful if you would not say anything until I have finished.'

Gabriella sat down. Her face was pale and her eyes heavy. Mrs Valencie appeared not to notice.

'Now I have some bad news.'

Gabriella lifted her eyes in query.

'Yes. Unfortunately your father's affairs were not as good as we thought. He has not left much money at all. It will have to be carefully managed.'

'My father led me to understand there would be plenty of money for us all. He promised to leave me some money,' said Gabriella, 'and I am certain he also would have provided for you and his step-daughters.'

'Your father has left everything to me, but there is very little money. Your father has taken this step because he believed it would be better managed by someone who has more experience and will take into account your best interests,' said Mrs. Valencie.

Gabriella inhaled sharply. 'That's not what he told me,' she said.

'Please,' said Mrs. Valencie in a louder tone. 'Let me explain. When it came to writing his will, your father took advice from his solicitor and has made proper arrangements. I am to oversee what small amount of money there is and I will invest it as wisely as possible. In the meantime we will have to economise as much as possible so that we have some security.

'First of all,' she continued, 'I am making changes in the household arrangements. Nanny and her husband are getting too old to cope with their duties and I cannot afford to pay them as well as new staff. Therefore, they will have to leave. I will then be able to afford new staff who will do twice the work.'

'But where will Nanny live?' asked Gabriella. 'And what pension can you give them?'

'I'm sure they have relatives they can go to. As to a pension, there is not enough money.'

'Madam, please, Nanny and Mr. Georges have worked for us most of their lives. Nanny brought me up when my mother died. I must do what I can for their future. All I can think is that I pay their wages from my allowance. Then if you really wish, you can take on new staff.'

'I'm afraid you do not realise the extent of the problem I have been left with,' said Mrs. Valencie. 'Your allowance will have to be cut. In fact, there is so little money that there will be times when I cannot give you any allowance at all. You will live here, of course, but your expenses must be curtailed as much as possible.'

Gabriella was not expecting this and the shock kept her quiet for a short time.

'Then you leave me with no choice, Madam,' said Gabriella. 'I know of no relatives Nanny can go to, nor can I expose her to the shame of living off charity. I, myself, will do whatever work Nanny and Mr. Georges cannot do. Between us we will do everything your new staff would do and more besides. You will not need to pay me but you will continue to pay Nanny her proper wages. This will be cheaper than taking on staff who would expect larger wages than are given to Nanny and Mr. Georges.'

It was clear that Mrs. Valencie had not thought of this solution to her problems

'I am not sure I can agree to this. I am by no means sure it will work. If you wish to help, that is your affair. I would, moreover, expect you to keep the standards up, and I do not see how you can do that.'

'I often helped Nanny after my mother died so I know what to do. I will do everything necessary to keep the standards as before.'

'Very well, I will give you a month's trial. If the service is not as I would expect Nanny and Mr. Georges will have to go.' There was just one point on which Mrs. Valencie needed assurance.

'If the extent of this arrangement were known to the neighbours, they would think the worst of me, therefore I expect you to keep the matter secret. It would be unfortunate if it became known that your father was a gambler and had lost a fortune by his ways.'

Gabriella gasped. 'My father did not gamble, Madam.'

'I'm sure this has come as a shock to you, as it did to me. I now have the extremely difficult task of making ends meet. We have been reduced to very straitened circumstances. If you really wish to help your old servants, it may solve another problem I have. Matilda and Florence each need their own rooms now that they are growing up. They cannot share anymore. They need room for their new clothes and room to prepare for the outings to the Palace which I believe are imminent. If you are to help in the house you will not be interested in visiting the Palace and will not need room for clothes or for dressing, so you will not mind giving up your bedroom to Florence. After all, there is a very good room at the top of the house. It's a little small maybe, but you will not need much room.'

* * *

Gabriella went up to her room. Her grief at her father's death was still hard to bear. She did not believe her stepmother's claims but did believe she was capable of spreading a rumour if it suited her. It made no difference to Gabriella if the neighbours knew what she was doing or not, so it would not be hard to keep her new manner of life quiet.

Gabriella stared at her reflection in the mirror, thought for a few moments, took in a deep breath and then changed her dress for an old one. She grabbed a coat and shoes and left the house by the kitchen door. The lake was not far away and walking had always been Gabriella's way of dealing with problems. She strode along the shore as fast as she could, hoping the wind in her face would brush away the tears.

She considered the problem and could find no alternative to what she had already decided. Nanny and her husband had no other home and no relatives at all. If they were turned out of the house they would be homeless. At their time of life they would not find work they would be able to do. Winter was well on the way and Gabriella shuddered to think what would become of her dear Nanny and Mr. Georges. They would most certainly refuse to allow Gabriella to accompany them when they had nowhere to go. Gabriella thought of giving then enough money to rent a small cottage and some for food. But if there would be times when Gabriella had no money at all, this would place Nanny in a dreadful situation, possibly facing eviction and the inevitable homelessness. The best thing to do was to help with the housework and that would give Gabriella time to come up with another solution.

After an hour of battling with the new situation Gabriella reluctantly turned back, knowing she must face the difficulties head on.

Gabriella entered the kitchen, put her coat in the small cloakroom, found an old apron in a cupboard and put it on.

'What are you doing, Miss Gabriella?' asked Nanny.

'I think it might help me if I did something,' said Gabriella. 'I'm going to help you a little. Now what will I do first?'

As the winter progressed Gabriella lit fires, swept and dusted rooms, carried hot water up to her step-sisters' rooms, carried the cold water back down, peeled potatoes and scrubbed vegetables, and on Mondays helped with the washing. Gabriella gave up eating with her step-family in the dining room and ate with Nanny instead. She had moved her few belongings to the cold room in the attic, but she no longer slept there. Instead she slept in the kitchen on a truckle bed, her aching body relieved a little by the heat from the stove.

At first both Matilda and Florence complained, despite having a warm room each.

'I want a real maid,' said Matilda. 'Gabriella does not do as I ask. Yesterday she refused to fetch my shoes from the cupboard.'

'She spilt water on my dressing table this morning and I had to mop it up with my handkerchief,' said Florence.

However Mrs. Valencie allowed Gabriella to do as she wished because she was saving a lot of money. It meant that Mrs. Valencie was able to buy her daughters a new gown each which she felt were necessary for the occasional visit to the Palace.

'So,' Mrs. Valencie told her daughters, 'you will stop grumbling and make the most of what I can give you. You will not mention Gabriella, or what she is doing, to anyone.'

* * *

Mr. Georges was butler in name only. His duties extended to cutting wood for the fires, scrubbing the kitchen floors, keeping the small garden clean and tidy and growing vegetables for the household. As a younger man he had enjoyed this aspect of his work outside in the sunshine. At that time his duties as a butler were very few. But Mrs.

Valencie expected the garden to supply much of their food and the garden became a heavy responsibility. So when the spring arrived Gabriella took to helping Mr. Georges with the kitchen garden. She dug the vegetable patch when she realised Mr. Georges no longer had the strength to do it. He helped her sow the seeds and showed her how to do things. These were happier times for Gabriella who, while out in the warm sunshine, took a few moments to listen to birdsong or to look at the view. A robin sat on her garden fork and kept her company.

Nanny looked on in great worry. Nothing she said could stop Gabriella from her work. All Nanny could do was make sure she ate properly. Fortunately, Gabriella knew she would have to eat to keep going and, although her appetite disappeared, she consumed everything Nanny put in front of her.

Nanny was puzzled but gave up trying to make sense of what was happening and concentrated on trying to relieve the burden of work on Gabriella's shoulders.

Chapter Five

One morning that spring Gabriella took the time, when she was sure her step mother and sisters would not find out, to visit her father's solicitor.

Mr. Browning welcomed her cautiously. 'Come in, come in, my dear. I'm not sure I can help you at all but do take a seat and tell me what concerns you.'

Gabriella entered the office and sat on a large leather chair placed before a big oak desk. The walls of the room were covered in old books and the floor piled with boxes.

'I would like to see my father's will, if you please, Mr. Browning.'

'I'm afraid I do not have it at present. I had to send it to a legal department in the city to be registered. You would not understand the wording if you were to read it anyway.'

'When will it be returned?'

'These things take time naturally and I would not expect to have it back for at least a year or maybe two.'

'Two years! Well, can you tell me exactly what was in it?'

'I think your step-mother has told you the contents. It is as she has told you. There was not so much money left as we had hoped. But I have given instructions for the money to be wisely invested so we hope that there will be enough to support the family as long as necessary. Your step-mother hopes to marry her daughters well, now they have good contacts. You too, of course. I was surprised to hear that you do not accompany the girls on their visits. But I think it will be to your advantage. Many will think the better of you for not going out in public so soon after your father's demise.'

Gabriella was hoping there had been a mistake with the will, so was disappointed. She found it hard to understand how her father could leave her in such difficulties. He had not given her any reason to think that something was wrong with his finances. Surely, she thought, he would have given her some indication if there was a problem.

Gabriella got up to leave but with a heavy heart. 'Please do not tell my step-mother I have been here. It could cause some problems at home.'

'I will not be seeing her for awhile anyway, so do not worry.' The old solicitor paused. 'Miss Gabriella, do you trust me?'

'I'm not sure.'

'Wise girl. But please be assured I am dealing with the situation. Do not give up hope. I will do everything I can to make things better.'

'Thank you,' she said and, pulling her hood over her head, she stepped out into the street.

* * *

When the solicitor saw her away he called for his clerk. The young man briskly entered the room and got ready a piece of paper and a pencil to write down his instructions.

'No, put that away, John,' said Mr. Browning. 'I want you to do something for me and I need it done as quietly as possible.'

'Yes, of course, sir.'

The solicitor explained he needed his clerk to travel to Derville, a city in Grelland, and make certain enquiries.

'As an excuse for going,' said the solicitor, 'you will say you are looking into various investment schemes for me. That is, if anyone asks. Do not go into details. Say it is confidential, but let something slip about investments. You may take some money with you. You will need to stay at an inn until you find what I am looking for. If you do not find it within a week come back, but do your best.'

John duly travelled to Derville. According to Mr. Browning's instructions regarding research into investments John visited the local bank. On the following day it would have been no surprise to anyone, should they be so interested, to see a solicitor's clerk enter the records office.

Chapter Six

Shortly thereafter, an event occurred which gave Roland, the young nobleman from Grelland, a change of heart concerning the kingship of Essenia. Since James was now appointed the heir Roland believed he was too late to change the situation. However, whilst out hunting with some acquaintances he strayed across the border into Essenia and, after chasing a deer into a woodland area, he fell off his horse into a shallow ravine. The ground was soft and he suffered no hurt except that his hand had landed on something sharp and it caused him some pain. It was a small irregular piece of metal, covered in mud. He put it in his pocket and thought no more about it until he got home and washed it.

The following week Roland went back to the ravine by himself. He took care to make sure no-one followed him. He found the place and undertook a search. He brushed away dead leaves and scraped the soil and rocks and, after an hour of finding nothing, Roland was about to give up. At the bottom of the ravine was a small stream and Roland went to wash his hands. The land was so steep that Roland slid the last few yards and his foot went into the stream and sank deeply into the mud at the edge. Roland removed his shoe in a bad temper and turned it upside down to empty out the water. There, stuck to the sole of his shoe, were several tiny particles glittering in the sunlight.

Roland had recently got into financial difficulties. It had

happened before but he had taken measures to cope at the time. Since then, he had inherited his father's small estate and, not having any turn for economy, had soon outrun his income. Without realising it he had got into debt again and now owed significant amounts to several tradesmen. His man of business suggested that he sell some of his assets to cope with the immediate embarrassments which Roland was forced to do. But Roland did not take to this new life of austerity. He was not used to it at all.

Back at home Roland visited the premises of a small scientific college. In particular, he searched for a professor of geology.

The professor, a white haired, bespectacled elderly man, asked a few questions but realised that Roland did not want to tell him much.

Roland asked him how one could be sure he had found gold and not something else.

'Do you have any samples for me to look at?' asked the professor.

Roland dug in his pocket and handed the professor a small piece.

'It certainly looks like gold,' said the professor. He took down a small vial from a shelf, poured a little of the liquid into a glass jar and added the sample. 'Yes. As you can see, it's gold.'

Roland looked at the scrap of gold in the jar. 'It's not doing anything.'

'No, it won't if it's gold. Iron pyrites would have dissolved by now. I can do more tests if you want but I'm certain you have a piece of gold here.'

Roland quickly suppressed the feeling of euphoria. 'It's interesting,' he said airily, 'but I doubt there's any more where that came from.'

'Probably not,' said the professor. 'Do call again if I can help with anything else.'

After Roland had left the professor went in search of the college Dean. 'Do you have a minute?' he asked after locating the Dean in the library.

'Of course,' said the Dean. 'Can we talk here or will we go to my office?'

'We might go to your office.'

The Dean looked interested. 'Come along then.'

'I've just had a visit from Roland,' said the professor, after sinking into an armchair beside the Dean's fire.

'Ah,' said the Dean. 'Go on.'

'The silly chump has found some gold and thinks he has discovered, excuse the pun, a gold mine.'

'And has he?'

'No. He tried hard to make me think he had been travelling in the north but I happen to know he has been south. To Essenia, actually.'

'And you think he has discovered gold in Essenia and will do something stupid in order to extract it.'

'Precisely. I know from historical reports that gold can be found in Essenia but always in such small quantities that it is not worth digging for. The amount found is never worth the time and effort needed to get it.'

'But you think that because it is in Essenia Roland may do something disastrous in order to lay claim to it. He's second in line to the throne there, isn't he?'

'Mm, yes. I just wonder what he is up to and if we can avert a diplomatic incident. The King wants to stay friendly with Essenia. Roland's reputation is not the best.'

'You mean that incident with the wealthy widow? Her husband died in mysterious circumstances, I believe.'

'Roland wanted to marry the widow after she inherited all that money but she was just amusing herself with him. She had enough sense not to marry him.'

'Nothing was ever proved against Roland, with regard to the husband's death, I mean?'

'No, the doctor was unsure as to the cause of death but in the end he had to write on the certificate that it was a heart problem. He suspected poison but could not prove it. There was a rumpus though, at one of the widow's evening events. Someone heard Roland tell the widow that he would expose her and she said that if he did he would be exposed too. But the witness was none too reliable, so it may not have been the exact words used. But shortly after that Roland was seen in a new carriage and, apparently, all his debts got paid. Mind you, he soon gathered a few more.'

'So you are worried he may be unscrupulous enough to do something about the gold in Essenia.'

'Yes, but what exactly he could do I cannot conjecture. Would it be expedient to inform the King?'

'It couldn't hurt.'

Meanwhile Roland was making plans to find the gold and keep it for himself. He had visions of untold wealth. He knew he could not buy the land on which he had found the gold. It belonged to the crown and any enquiries he made as to purchasing the land would make the King wonder why he wanted it. The King might then find the gold for himself. The role of the Essenian King began to look very attractive and since Roland was second in line to the throne he began to view it as his right.

To further his schemes, Roland looked again at the documents outlining his parentage to see if he could find that he was closer to the throne of Essenia than James. The page containing Roland's genealogy was complicated. He had to refer to other pages to check James's lineage and see how it connected to his own. The results were dispiriting. Roland was further from the throne than he had expected.

Roland was related to the King of Grelland because his father had descended from a brother of the King's great-grandmother on Roland's grandmother's side. He was also distantly related to the present King of Essenia because his grandmother had been an aunt of the King. But James's grandmother had been an older aunt of the King's and James's father had descended from a brother of Grelland's King's grandfather. Roland's head hurt so he nearly gave up on his ancestors.

Roland searched further back to see if his great-grandmother had any other royal connections that would further his ambitions but there were none. But he made one discovery which he believed he could exploit.

Chapter Seven

The Queen took on her new job with a willing heart and great enthusiasm. There were two young maids in the household, Jenny, the scullery maid, and Nell, the chamber maid. In time Jenny overcame her shyness and helped with good advice because she had assisted the cook on many occasions. The Queen soon promoted Jenny to kitchen and parlour maid. Nell, the chamber maid, found the blossoming friendship between the Queen and the former scullery maid to be most unusual. Quite often Nell would find the Queen and Jenny drinking tea together and discussing recipes. Nell was not sure how to deal with this until one morning the Queen caught sight of Nell peeping into the kitchen from the scullery.

'Ah Nell,' said the Queen, 'I'm pleased to see you. Come and have tea with us. We are trying to decide what to have for dinner. Maybe you have some suggestions. Did you do any cooking at home?' And with questions like these the two girls embraced the new regime in the kitchen and began to feel very important to the running of the Palace.

The Queen viewed her work as a calling and set out to make everyone happy with her culinary expertise. However, it took a while before such expertise became apparent and the cooking was a little unpredictable.

For breakfast the King either crunched burnt toast or chewed warm bread. Lunches were edible because the

Queen made sandwiches from fresh bread and local cheese, delivered daily from the town. She threw in whatever salad the gardener could find. At dinner time the occupants of the Palace manfully chewed through their stew and hard dumplings or chiselled the pastry off the apple pie. The flavours were odd at times as the Queen experimented with those vegetables which happened to be in season.

The gardener realised that whatever vegetables he gave to the Queen she threw into the pot indiscriminately. So he took to asking Jenny what was for dinner before he delivered anything. The meals improved.

The King stated his health was much better, which he put down to the large amount of herbs in his lunchtime sandwiches. He said how much he appreciated his good wife's efforts. The rest of the Palace personnel took their lead from him. James said that after eating a bowl of the Queen's porridge he no longer got hungry long before lunch. Whereas before he always got hungry by ten o'clock in the morning, he now lasted until eleven. The Secretary said the trouble he had been having with his teeth and gums was now cured. The gardener, having chewed his food well, said he did not get indigestion anymore and how wonderful it all was. Jenny, the kitchen/parlour maid, glowed as she shared her mistress's praise. She decided she would try to get better bargains from the merchants at the market. Nell cleared the plates after each meal confident that everyone had been well fed.

Encouraged by the comments, the Queen conjured up large and solid omelettes, roasts of which some were well done and some rare, and soups of unusual combinations. When time allowed, she baked heavy cakes. No one went hungry.

* * *

On receiving an invitation to visit the Queen for afternoon

tea, Mrs Rosaria Rodriguez gave certain instructions to her cook. Mrs Rodriguez had been informed of the new arrangement with regard to the cooking.

Thus one afternoon Mrs. Rodriguez entered the Palace with a large tin under her arm.

'Ah, Rosaria,' said the Queen smiling. 'I'm delighted you could come. I have a cake in the oven but unfortunately it seems to be taking longer to cook than I thought. But never mind, we can have tea while we wait.'

'It's lovely to see you too, Eleanor,' said Mrs. Rodriguez. 'As to the cake, I have brought one or two little samples for you to try. I am hoping you and the King will be kind enough to have dinner with me soon. My cook was nervous about what you might like, so made a few little things and asked that you please tell her which you like best so she can cook it for you when you come.'

The Queen suspected an ulterior motive but was delighted to see a large array of desserts in the tin. 'Thank you, dear Rosaria. I won't have to cook a pudding tonight, that's for sure.'

The Queen settled her guest beside the fire and poured some tea. 'Now, what I want to know is this: what is the situation with Gabriella? As you know, her father rendered us great help last year with the floods and I would like to help Gabriella if I can.'

'I cannot tell you much. When I recently spent an afternoon with Mrs. Valencie, Gabriella only came into the room once and that was to bring the tea tray. I must admit I was shocked by Mrs. Valencie's manner. She spoke to Gabriella sharply and told her the sugar was missing. Then she seemed to remember that I was present. So she changed her tone and asked Gabriella nicely if she wouldn't mind getting some sugar, "there's a good girl".'

'Oh dear,' said the Queen.

'Yes, I'm wondering what the set-up is there now. I had

the feeling Gabriella is taking over some of Nanny's duties. I know Nanny is getting old now but I don't know why Mrs. Valencie doesn't hire a new servant. I'm sure the expense would be well within her income.'

The Queen pondered the problem and said that discreetly she would try to find out what the situation was. In the meantime they tried some of the lovely cakes in the tin.

The next day the Queen was able to write a short note to Mrs Rodriguez to thank her for the provisions.

'The King and I both loved the chocolate cake. James said they were all delicious, which they were, but the other day he also said that about my apple pie and I know for certain it was not one of my best!'

Chapter Eight

James quickly settled into his new position and soon realised there were several problems besetting the Palace. He was not sure how to tackle this but asked for an appointment with the King's Secretary.

'As you know, Mr. Secretary,' said James, 'I was to have worked my way up in my uncle's business. I had already spent time as the office boy and messenger and was supposed to start in the accounts office this year. I wonder if I can approach this matter of the King's work in the same way. For instance, I would like to spend a few weeks with each of the Palace departments to get an idea of what problems they encounter. Then maybe I could work for a few weeks in the Treasury or with the Guard.'

The Secretary was impressed by James's intelligence and general willingness to learn. He said he would discuss it with the King. The King was delighted with the idea but said he did not want James to feel he had to tire himself out.

'You see,' said the King, 'James will also have to learn to be comfortable in the company of dignitaries and when he attends our rare evening banquets I do not want him to fall asleep at the table.'

The Secretary privately thought that James was young and healthy enough to cope with everything but said he would arrange a schedule which would take everyone's wishes into account. The Treasury and the Guard occupied small buildings in the city just three miles to the south of the Palace and those in charge welcomed the Mr. Secretary's suggestions and quickly made arrangements for the Prince to visit.

Thus life went on gently.

At the end of the autumn the King of Grelland decided to send Roland to Essenia on a mission of goodwill. The King had been informed by his advisers of Roland's interest in gold. But he did not believe a simple visit of goodwill to Essenia could give Roland an opportunity for any mischief, and the King was hoping that Roland would benefit from taking on more responsibility. In due course the King of Essenia got a letter from that young nobleman, Roland, indicated the reasons for a visit. Roland wrote that naturally he was delighted to be able to accede to the wishes of his King and hoped that December would be a convenient time. He added, almost as an afterthought, that he would be most grateful if Prince James would meet him and conduct his party to the Palace in case they missed their way. Places to meet were suggested.

The King showed the letter to James. The King believed it would be a good experience for James to undertake this small errand and taught him how to greet the expected party and how to behave generally. A proper reception for Roland would be held when he arrived at the Palace.

* * *

Life went by swiftly for Gabriella. In late summer Gabriella and Nanny had taken time to pick berries in the woods. It had given Gabriella a few hours to come to terms with her new life, time to breathe fresh air and, for a moment of two, to forget her hard work. She turned brown in the sunshine.

Autumn gave way to winter and the first flurries of snow fell on the high hills.

It happened that on an evening in December, Gabriella,

having finished her duties for the day, was resting before the last of the fire in the kitchen. A knock on the door startled her. Mr. Georges went to answer it and invited the caller in.

'It's William Gilbert, Nanny,' announced Mr. Georges.

Gabriella was surprised to see the head groom from the Palace stables and he was no less surprised to see her in the kitchen.

'I am sorry to disturb you, Miss. I wasn't expecting you to be here but if you could help me I would be most grateful.'

'Good evening, Mr. Gilbert. Please come and sit beside the fire,' said Gabriella.

Nanny got up to fetch their visitor a cup of tea.

'No, I cannot stay,' said William Gilbert. 'I don't think you can help but the Prince has gone missing. Now, because Miss Gabriella and the Prince used to know each other well, I wondered if you had heard or seen anything of him. We are extremely worried. The Prince was to have met a party of travellers but when these travellers arrived, James was not with them and they had not seen him at all.'

Gabriella felt her stomach go into cramps. 'No, we have not seen him nor have we heard of anything unusual. But please tell me what I can do to help.'

'Nothing at all, Miss,' he said. 'His horse is back in the stable but there was no rider with it. I must admit to feeling anxious. I had better get off now and search somewhere else. I'll have to deal with the horse later too. He came back in such a bad state. His mane is all tied up in knots.'

'I beg your pardon Mr. Gilbert, but what did you say?'

'I have to get going Miss, I'm afraid, to search elsewhere.'

'No, not that. What about the horse? Did you say there were knots in the mane? How many knots were there?'

'Three or four, Miss. I was more worried about the young lad being missing than the state of the horse. It was odd though. The horse's mane wasn't in knots because of simply being messed up. It looked as if someone had carefully tied the knots.'

'Then I think I know where James is. How quickly can you get back to the stables to check the number of knots?'

'It's only five minutes away, Miss, as you know but I don't really understand how it can help.'

'I don't have time to explain now. Please go as quickly as you can and bring back some really warm clothes with you and whatever extra coats or blankets you can carry. Please be quick. I will get ready in the meantime.'

'Well, if you're sure, Miss,' said the groom. 'I expect you know better than I do and anything is worth a try. Will I bring anyone else with me?'

'No, we'll be quicker on our own,' said Gabriella. 'Please hurry.'

* * *

Gabriella went to get her warmest clothes from the cloakroom, trying to quell Nanny's fears at the same time. She fetched a scarf, a hat, a thick coat with a hood to put over the hat, warm gloves and heavy boots.

'Please do not go out in this bitter cold, Gabriella,' pleaded Nanny.

'I must, Nanny. You know I must. I'm used to going out in colder weather than this.'

'Yes, I know, but it's dark. What would happen if you got lost?'

'Nanny, I know every tree and rock for miles. I won't get lost. Is there any of that soup left? And can you put it in something so I can carry it with me? I'll wrap it in a blanket to keep it warm. I'll be gone for a while so don't wait up for me.'

They bustled around and by the time the groom returned Gabriella was ready to go.

'You look like a plum pudding,' said Nanny.

Gabriella laughed. 'At least I won't get cold. I'll probably get too hot once we start walking.'

Slightly cheered by this remark, Nanny waved them off before shutting the door. She went to the store cupboard to fetch vegetables to make more soup, in an effort to keep busy.

William Gilbert had brought a lantern with him and a bag of extra clothes. 'There were three knots, Miss, and very tightly tied they were too.'

'Good,' said Gabriella as he walked ahead of Mr. Gilbert. 'Then I know exactly where James is.'

'There's a bit of a moon, now that snow shower has stopped, so we don't really need this lantern.'

'We'll need it when we get where we are going.'

'And where are we going, Miss?'

'To the other side of the lake.'

'But Miss Gabriella, it will take us at least two hours to walk around there.'

'We're not going to walk,' said Gabriella. 'We're taking a boat.'

'In the dark, Miss? Surely not. We'll end up on that rock which sticks up in the middle.'

'Mr. Gilbert,' said Gabriella, 'I spent my childhood on this lake. We won't hit the rock. It's a good thing it snowed because that rock is now white. We'll be able to see it easily. Quickly now, please.'

They got to the lake shore and Gabriella climbed into an old boat. 'Loose the boat and jump in.'

'The other boat is lighter, Miss.'

'I know this boat better and it has two sets of oars. Please hurry.'

'You're not thinking of rowing, Miss?'

'Of course I am. Push us away, if you please. We've no time to lose.'

William got in, grabbed an oar and pushed the boat away

from the small jetty. He sat himself behind Gabriella. 'You set the pace, Miss.'

Gabriella dug her oars into the water and they set off.

'Can you tell me exactly where we're going?' asked William.

'Three knots means that cave on the far edge of the lake,' said Gabriella in between pulling on her oars. 'It's a game we played as children. One of us would pretend to be lost and would send the pony home with knots in his mane. Each number of knots meant a different location. If James was pretending to be lost, Peter and I had to work out where he was and rescue him. I was supposed to bring sandwiches . . .'

'Save your breath,' said William. 'I get the idea. Let me row for a while on my own.'

'No I'm fine. I'll be warmer if I work, but I'll stop talking.'

They pulled together, adjusting their course occasionally. It took them twenty minutes to reach the rock.

'Which side of the rock do we go?' asked William.

'To the west. It's deeper.'

'And how do you know that, Miss?'

'Just another game we played. We were pirates chasing a galleon and had to take soundings to avoid hitting the rock.'

'Of course,' said William and he smiled to himself.

William pulled on one oar until they were pointed in the right direction. Gabriella was getting tired but anxiety kept her going. 'Not much further now. My hands are getting cold.'

Gabriella was glad when the boat scrunched on the far shore.

'I'm not absolutely certain James will be in the cave. He might be anywhere, but at least he should be in this area.' Gabriella tied her scarf a little tighter and pulled her coat closer to her and set out to search.

They looked in the cave but he was not there. 'I'll look behind the cave,' said Gabriella. 'Do you want to go the other way, Mr. Gilbert?'

'No, lass, we'll stay together now. I can't risk losing you as well as the Prince.'

They climbed the short incline above the cave looking all ways. They soon walked into a wooded area.

'I'm worried we might be in the wrong place,' said Gabriella. 'What if James is along the shore of the lake? He could be anywhere. These trees make it harder to see for any distance.'

'I'll call, Miss, 'said William. He shouted into the breeze.

'Hush, listen,' said Gabriella. They heard a soft call close by, headed towards it, and before long found James. He was shivering badly, rolled up in a tight ball beside a tree. His foot was bound with a chain to the tree.

'Whatever has happened here,' cried William. 'Can you do something to help the poor boy to be a little warmer, Miss? I'll find a stone to break this chain.'

William had to walk to the shore of the lake to find two stones large enough for the purpose. Gabriella, who was crying by now, wrapped James up in the extra blankets and gave him some soup from the bottle Nanny had given her. Her fingers were shaking with the fright.

James was still trembling from head to toe but took the soup gladly. 'Thank goodness you are here,' he said, his voice quivering with the cold. 'I thought I was going to die.'

'Oh, do not think of such a thing,' said Gabriella. 'Drink this and as soon as Mr. Gilbert has you free we must be away.'

William put one of the stones on the far side of the tree, laid the chain on it and hit it hard several times with the other stone. He soon broke through the links. 'You'll have to walk with that bit of chain still attached to your ankle for now. We can get the blacksmith to cut through it tomorrow in the light. Lean on me now and we'll be off home.'

James's legs were so stiff with cold he could hardly move them but he got to the boat by hanging onto both William and Gabriella. Gabriella was laughing with relief now. 'We must look an odd sight,' she said. 'If anyone saw us they'd think we were a very strange animal.' James tried to laugh but it stuck in his throat.

William helped James and Gabriella into the boat, got himself in safely and shoved off.

Gabriella fiddled about with a large triangle of fabric which had been rolled around a thin mast and left lying on the floor of the boat. She propped the mast up in a makeshift holder at the stern. The lower edge of the triangle was attached to a thin beam which extended over the side of the boat. A piece of wood jutting up from the side prevented the beam from blowing forwards.

'What are you doing, Miss?' asked William.

'Peter made this a few years ago. It was the nearest thing we could get to a sail. It only works if the wind is in the same direction you want to go, which it is at the moment. It will help us a little bit and give James some shelter too.'

Gabriella and William took the oars up again. 'Keep that blanket over your head, Master James, and don't fall asleep. Keep talking to us.' said William. 'We're not home and dry yet.'

William tried to keep the Prince awake with questions, but James was not very coherent.

'You must keep awake, Master James,' said William. 'Tell us what happened.'

James mumbled something about being caught in a trap, being tied up and gagged and a bag being put over his head. 'I couldn't do a thing to stop them. There must have been two of the ruffians. They put me back on the horse and took me into the forest. The next thing I knew they threw me on the ground and rode off. I don't think I can talk any more. My mouth is frozen up.'

'You must keep trying,' said William. 'What happened next.'

James's teeth were chattering. 'When they went, I realised

I was tied to a tree. I got the bag off my head by snagging it on the tree trunk. It took me ages to free myself of the ropes around my hands. I couldn't do anything about the chain though. For some reason they left my horse. He came to me when I called. I took off the rug under the saddle. Oh yes, we'll have to go back for the saddle tomorrow.'

'Don't worry about that,' said William. 'Go on.'

'I tied the knots in the horse's mane. I had no real expectation of you realising what they were for, but it was the only thing I could think of. Then I sent him home. There was nothing else I could do. I got colder and colder and . . .' But James could go no further

Gabriella said she would explain to James how she found out about the knots when she got her breath back.

The return journey was quicker. Getting James to Gabriella's house was not easy because they were all exhausted, but they made it and, with huge relief, stepped into the doorway.

Nanny had not gone to bed. She said she could not sleep while Gabriella was out on such a night. The fire had been rekindled and was burning warmly. There was hot milk in a jug on the hearth and a kettle boiling on the stove.

They bundled James into the armchair nearest the fire and gave him a hot drink. Within minutes he was asleep. Nanny fetched another blanket and wrapped it round his feet.

'I think he'll be all right now,' said Gabriella, 'but he'll have to stay here until morning. Do you want to stay as well, Mr. Gilbert? There's a spare room we can get ready for you if you wish.'

'No, Miss, thank you. I'll just warm myself through with some hot tea, if you don't mind, then I must get a message to the Palace. Others will be searching and the Queen will be fretting. The King was going to get the Guard out at first light.'

'I'll sit up with the young man in case he gets a fever

during the night,' said Nanny. She fetched some soup for Gabriella.

Gabriella saw William to the door and came back to tell Nanny the story in between mouthfuls of soup. 'We won't find out much more about the situation until morning, but I'm so tired I think I could sleep for a week.'

Chapter Nine

The previous evening Roland had arrived at the Palace with two servants who acted as body guards. After being presented to the King, Roland gave him letters from the King of Grelland. Roland asked after James.

'I thought he was with you,' said the King.

'We arrived at the meeting point but James was not there. We waited for some time but thought it best to come directly to the Palace. An innkeeper gave us directions. Are you sure James is not here?'

A search was made but James was nowhere to be found. The King gave instructions to as many of his staff as could be spared to search everywhere they could.

'My men will help,' said Roland. 'I would be grieved if we were the cause of any mishap to James.'

The King protested but half-heartedly. In truth he was grateful for any help.

'My men will retrace our steps and search along the way until they get back to the meeting place,' said Roland. 'I'm sure we will find James safe and well.'

Roland's henchmen set off, but curiously did not go too far. Knowing full well where James was they found an inn and ate a good meal.

* * *

James woke to find Nanny stirring something on the stove

and Gabriella laying a table. He assumed that Gabriella was in the kitchen because of the emergency. It was still dark outside so he guessed it was early.

Gabriella noticed him wake up. 'Good morning,' she said. 'How are you?'

'I ache to high heaven. I'm stiff but I think I can move.'

'I'll take a look at you before you do,' said Nanny. She felt his forehead and checked his pulse. 'Not too bad,' she conceded.

James thought he had gone back to the nursery. 'I'll be fine, Nanny, thank you.'

'Come to the table then, and take some hot tea.'

'Do you feel well enough to tell us what happened?' asked Gabriella when he was settled.

'It was most odd. I was on my way to meet some people from Grelland, just a small group. There was a cottage by the side of the road and two men on horses came out from behind it and took me by surprise. They rode either side of me and one grabbed my horse's bridle and the other threw a bag over my head. I was so shocked I didn't have time to do anything about it.'

Gabriella said nothing but waited while James took a sip of his tea.

'They must have had a rope ready because I felt it pin my arms to my sides and then they wrapped it round and round so that I couldn't move at all. I couldn't see anything, of course. We rode off for some distance and then I was taken off the horse and pushed to the ground. They put something round my ankle but I didn't know what it was at that moment. Then they left. I waited until it was really quiet and tried to move.'

Nanny ladled some porridge into a bowl, poured cream over the top and handed it to James with a jar of honey.

'I found that if I wriggled I could loosen the ropes on my shoulders. It took me about half an hour but eventually I got all the ropes off over my head. It was getting dark of course, but I knew where I was immediately. I know that part of the country like the back of my hand. My horse was standing close by too.'

'Were you not cold by then?' asked Gabriella.

'The wriggling had kept me warm but I knew it would get colder as the night went on.'

'How long did it take you to think of the knots?'

'Another hour, I'm afraid. I tried hard to get out of that chain they put round the tree. If I got free I needed my horse to get me home. But nothing worked. I looked in the saddle bags but the thieves had taken anything I could have used to write a note with. My money was gone but I did not have that much with me anyway.'

James paused to eat some porridge. 'This is good, thank you,' he said and ate some more. 'I'd forgotten porridge could taste like this.'

Gabriella waited patiently.

'In the end I thought of the knots. They were my last hope. I did not really think they would work. The horse did not want to go and it took me a while to make him go home. I knew William would not know of our games when we were children but there was a chance he would ask you if you had seen me, which it seems he did.'

'Yes, he did.'

'I thought you would tell him where I was and leave it to him to find me.'

'No,' said Gabriella.

'No, of course not. Well, time went by and I did get cold, really cold. I have no idea how long it was. I kept trying to keep warm, but in the end I got so tired that I just curled up in a ball and hoped I would survive until the morning. Then I heard someone calling. You can't imagine the relief.'

There was a gentle knock on the door. Gabriella opened it a little and then wider when she saw Mr. Gilbert.

'I have the pony and trap outside,' said William. 'It was thought best to take the Prince home before Mrs. Valencie rises.'

'Yes, of course,' said Gabriella. 'James will be ready in a few minutes. Nanny says he does not have a fever but we cannot risk him getting cold again. Once he has eaten this hot food we think he will be fit enough.'

Nanny gave William hot tea and a bowl of porridge. He asked if James had told them any more of what had happened.

'It seems he was attacked by a couple of masked robbers, but he cannot understand why they tied him to that tree. They had to drag him a long way off his path to get there too. It's all most odd,' said Gabriella.

'I tried to get this chain off my foot but I cut my ankle doing it,' said James

'I've padded the chain with a towel,' said Nanny, 'but you will have to get it off as quickly as you can and get the doctor to look at that bad cut. I've dressed it but the doctor will know best.'

'I must thank you both so much,' said James. 'If you had not come to rescue me I do not think I could have survived. It was so cold.'

Gabriella said she could not bear to think about it. James looked at her and changed the subject. He asked William if all was well at the Palace and if Roland had arrived. William took the hint, said all was well and that the weather was better now it was morning.

When Nanny had James wrapped up in a thick coat and hat she said he might survive the short journey, but William was to make sure the doctor saw James that very morning.

'The Queen has already sent for the doctor who will be waiting for him to arrive.'

James said thank you many times and said he would contact then when he felt better. He shook Gabriella's hand. She laughed. 'At least your hand is warmer than last night.

Oh, and just for now, I would be most grateful if you did not mention this matter to anyone, particularly to Mrs. Valencie.'

James began to wonder what sort of life Gabriella was leading.

* * *

Back at the Palace, the King and Queen realised how fond they were of their protégé, and were delighted to have him home safely. The Queen whisked James up to his room where a fire was burning and the doctor was waiting.

The doctor took his time examining his patient. He exclaimed in surprise when he saw the chain around the Prince's ankle, but he was able to re-dress the cut on his ankle and ask the Queen what could be done to get that chain off. The Queen said the blacksmith was to visit later that morning when they hoped James would be well enough to visit the stables where the chain could be removed without causing any more injury and before too many rumours circulated.

Downstairs, the first thing the King did was to ask Mr. Secretary to call the Captain of the Guard. Within ten minutes the Captain was shown into the King's library.

'I believe you have been informed of the attack upon Prince James,' said the King.

'Yes, Sir,' said the Captain. 'The Guard has been ready and waiting for instructions since dawn.'

'Good,' said the King. 'This is a most disgraceful episode. We need to get to the bottom of it quickly. If we let this sort of thing go on, people will start locking their doors just to go to market. Now do you have any suggestions?'

'Yes, Sir. I would be grateful to be able to interview the Prince to ascertain exactly where he was attacked and then set my company to search for evidence along the way. I will also send some of the guardsmen to question people living in the area to see what we can discover.'

'A good plan. Now, I want your best officer in charge of looking for clues. I don't want a lot of men on horses destroying the evidence.'

'Of course, Sir. I have a young officer in mind. He has proved very capable.'

'Very well, then. Come with me to see the Prince.'

They found James wrapped in blankets, seated in an armchair before a large fire. The Queen and the doctor were putting the finishing touches to a dressing on James's ankle.

'How are you, dear boy?' asked the King.

'I'm recovering well, Sir, under the best of care.'

The Queen smiled.

The King asked the doctor if James would be well enough to talk for a few minutes. Privately the doctor thought James's constitution would survive far worse but he was aware the Queen thought James would catch pneumonia and die unless he received careful nursing for at least a month.

'Now then,' considered the doctor, 'I don't want my patient excited at all or talking for too long but I think he will be able to talk for a short while.' He gave the Queen instructions for James's further care.

The Queen remembered she had to cook breakfast for everyone including a guest, so hurried to the kitchen, accompanying the doctor to the door on her way.

James carefully removed several blankets, wiped a few beads of sweat off his brow and gave his attention to the Captain.

After the Captain left, the King told James he wanted to send for Gabriella to thank her but James dissuaded him saying she wanted to keep the matter quiet. On reflection the King thought it was the best course but would think of some way to show their appreciation for her courageous efforts. Both James and the King thought there were some odd features of the robbery and the matter made the King very uneasy.

Down in the kitchen the Queen was overseeing breakfast but her mind was obviously elsewhere. Jenny rescued some sausages before they caught fire and threw out some toast which had. Jenny took the best of the offerings to the dining room where she found the King in deep thought by the window.

Roland entered the dining room and instantly enquired after James. The King said he was pleased to report that James had come home safely. He did not give any details but was startled when he caught a strange look on Roland's face. 'Are your servants back yet?' the King inquired. 'They will be looked after by our staff. I'm sorry James is not able to welcome you but we hope he will be at dinner with us tonight.'

Roland recovered his demeanour and said if it would be convenient he would visit the stables after breakfast and see what had happened to his servants. He hoped that no mishap had overtaken James. The King did not reply.

The King asked how things were going along in Grelland in an attempt to keep a light conversation going. Roland was struggling with crispy sausages and thankfully laid down his fork to answer.

* * *

Sometime later Roland casually strolled into the stable and found his servants rubbing down their horses. After making sure no-one else was around, Roland asked what had happened.

The two men shuffled about uncomfortably. 'As soon as it was light this morning we went back to that place where we left him, but there was nothing there,' said one in a hoarse whisper. 'We were expecting him to have died in the cold, and we would have taken off the ropes and the chain and left him for someone else to find. No-one would have known how he had died. But it didn't work out that way. Someone had obviously been lying in the snow but there was no sign of a body or of the chain. We searched around in case the Prince had got free and was lying somewhere else or had been able to take shelter somewhere, but we couldn't find any trace of him at all. We looked for the chain too in case he'd been able to remove it, but there was nothing at all. We had to come back here and pretend we had been looking all night along our route.' The men did not tell Roland of the length of chain still attached to the tree or the two stones which had mysteriously appeared by the tree.

'You seem to have made a real mess of the whole thing,' said Roland angrily.

'You don't pay us enough for this sort of work,' began the other servant, but before he could continue Roland heard someone coming and told them to act normally and take their breakfast in the kitchen. He would speak to them again later. He walked out to find a blacksmith setting up his tools. He did not connect the smith to his problem and so walked back to the Palace.

* * *

The Queen asked Nell if she would be kind enough to clear up while Jenny helped with another matter.

'We are needed upstairs,' said the Queen to Jenny.

As they entered James's room, he got out of his chair awkwardly.

'We need to help the Prince to the stables, Jenny, if you please,' said the Queen who by this time, tired from lack of sleep and worry, felt tears fill her eyes.

'I have hold of him, Ma'am,' said Jenny. 'Don't worry.'

'Oh,' moaned James. 'Oh, oh.' His groans spluttered into

laughter. 'I must take advantage of this. I think I'll be injured for a week.'

'I believe, Ma'am,' said Jenny firmly, 'that his highness is able to walk on his own.'

'I am indeed,' said James. 'But I am most grateful to you both. I would be far worse without the sympathy.' He bent to pick up the end of the chain. 'I had better carry this or someone will think we have a ghost.'

The Queen gave him a lopsided grin, but dried her tears.

The blacksmith was skilled enough to get the chain off without further injury. He wondered what was going on but the Queen had asked him to be quiet about the matter so he left it at that.

Chapter Ten

James recovered quickly and, apart from a slight limp, came to dinner as if nothing bad had happened. He greeted Roland with courtesy and spent a short time greeting each of the other guests the Queen had invited. The dining room was full. Gabriella was amongst them but she gave no indication that she had spent her previous night rescuing the Prince.

Mrs. Valencie had struggled to come to terms with the Palace's invitation to Gabriella. She thought about it and decided her reputation would be better served by Gabriella's attendance than by her absence. On many occasions in the past Mrs. Valencie had been embarrassed to see how other guests compared Gabriella to Matilda and Florence. Nobody was rude enough to say anything but Gabriella had always been received with greater warmth and kindness than her own daughters. So Mrs. Valencie dressed her two daughters in large gowns, bought as cheaply as possible, but did not purchase any new ones for Gabriella. If anything, this tactic had the opposite effect to that wanted.

Gabriella looked beautiful in anything. Her long dark hair shone, her blue eyes were clear and bright, her figure slim and well balanced. Matilda and Florence, both with mousy, dull hair, had a tendency to be plump, which was emphasised by the elaborate dresses. Matilda's nose was too big and Florence's face was flat. None of this would have mattered if the two sisters had been happy characters. But their overall bearing was moody and irritable. Gabriella stood out as being calm and elegant and, although a little too quiet, she was able to put her own problems to the back of her mind and pay attention to the concerns of others.

Roland was of great interest to all the young ladies. He was shorter than James but more darkly handsome. At times he was sarcastic and liked to gossip. Some young ladies found him exciting. James was thought to have the kinder character but Roland, due to the opulent way he dressed, appeared to have more money.

Roland did not pay any attention to Gabriella. He did not know who she was because James deliberately did not introduce her to him. Matilda and Florence ignored Gabriella for the evening and were pleased to see that she spent most of her time in conversation with the older members of the party. At dinner Gabriella had been seated as far from Roland as was possible and she found herself next to Mr. Secretary who chatted to her about the weather and plans for flood defences.

In her off-guarded moments Gabriella looked at James with great fondness. James too, whenever his polite duties allowed, was far more relaxed telling Gabriella about his mistakes while learning the ways of the Palace or about the intricacies of the Treasury. James knew he owed Gabriella his life and wished he could tell everyone.

James did not want to remind Gabriella of the previous night's work but he was concerned to discover if she had suffered any ill effects. After the dinner, everyone congregated in the large drawing room and James, seeing Gabriella in a quiet corner of the room, took her a cup of tea.

'How are you?' he asked, genuinely concerned.

'I am very well, James, thank you. A little tired maybe, but one good night's sleep will put that right.' She smiled. 'I am pleased to see that you have recovered well. It's good to be warm, isn't it?'

'Very,' said James. He noticed Gabriella shiver slightly and hoped to distract her thoughts. 'So what do you think of our company?'

'Your visiting dignitary is very flamboyant. If we continue to get visitors like this we will have to change our fashions to suit. We cannot have foreigners thinking we are behind the times in Essenia.'

James laughed. 'Please do not change the way you dress, Gabriella. Our visitors need to be set a good example.'

'Thank you, kind Sir,' Gabriella laughed quietly. 'Oh, and I understand the Queen cooked for the guests tonight. It was all very grand. I was so pleased that I did not have to cook today.'

'Do you do the cooking then?' asked James, surprised. 'I believe the Queen enjoys it, but we are trying to make people believe we have a large staff in the kitchen.'

Gabriella realised she had said more than she should have done. 'I do a little, but Nanny does most of it. Anyone would believe the kitchen staff here had a lot of help to produce that lovely banquet.'

'Our old cook sent her two nieces to do some of the work. I, myself, will be spending some weeks in the kitchen soon, to learn the ways of the staff here. If the next banquet is inedible, you will know that I had a hand in it.'

Gabriella smiled and looked so lovely that quietly, and without anyone seeing, James took Gabriella's hand and held it gently for a moment before he had to leave her to speak to others.

At the end of the evening the Queen called for everyone's attention and said she had an announcement to make.

'We have not had time yet to honour our new Prince on his arrival at the Palace, so we are arranging a small celebration to be held in July next year. You are all to be invited.' There was a murmur of appreciation. 'I will send you invitations in due time but I hope this advanced notice gives us all something to which we can look forward. Thank you all very much for giving us the pleasure of your company this evening.'

The Queen had timed the July party for the glut of vegetables which would be in the Palace gardens. She planned to keep expenses down by cooking gallons of soup and making large salads. The young people wanted to know what sort of party it was to be and were delighted to know that it was to be a ball.

While Roland's visit lasted James was unable to continue with his schedule. Instead, the King asked him to take Roland and some other young people to places of interest. Being December, James found it hard to fill the days. The young men preferred sporting activities to visiting old castles and the young ladies soon grew cold and had to be taken to tearooms. James found these girls extremely delicate. James was disappointed that, although Miss Matilda and Miss Florence attended, Gabriella did not accompany him on these expeditions. Her company would have made light work of the trips. The King insisted James take two or three officers from the Guard with him on his outings, stating that if there were robbers abroad the young people needed to be protected. The King may have had other reasons for this action but did not state what they were. James found it hard to juggle the whole party, but gave in with a good grace.

* * *

Towards the end of Roland's visit the Queen organised a small informal dance for the young people. In the bustle of preparations James was sent up the back stairs to bring down some extra chairs for the small band of musicians hired for the occasion. As he descended the stairs carrying two chairs he thought he heard a footstep behind him. His experience in the woods had made him nervous. There should not have been anyone else on that stairwell. James knew where everyone else was, so he quietly stepped onto a landing half way down the stairs, held the chairs in front of him, blew out the candle lighting the way and waited.

Someone was stealthily creeping down the stairs toward him. As the person drew level, James quickly lowered his chairs and pushed them forwards. Suddenly there was a lot of noise. Whoever had been coming down the stairs swore, but was unable to stop himself falling down the stairs, tangled hopelessly in chair legs. The crash brought everyone running. The light from the opened doors revealed a large man lying on the floor with two broken chairs on top of him. A dagger was sticking out of his leg.

James came down the stairs in a hurry but had to wait for two of the hired servants to remove the chairs. The King was called, who called the Secretary, who organised a stretcher for the injured man. The servants helped to remove the man to a bedroom in the servants' quarters. The stable boy was sent to fetch the doctor. Jenny ran to fetch William Gilbert to help clear up the mess at the foot of the stairs. She did not want Nell to faint at the sight of it.

The King found out the man was one of Roland's servants. Anxiously the King took his Secretary and James into his private rooms to ask what had happened. Hearing the story the King became angry.

'There is something seriously wrong here. I am going to have to take measures to prevent anything like this happening again. But I cannot have a diplomatic incident until I have positive proof that the man was up to no good. So, Mr. Secretary, how do you suggest we handle this situation?'

They came up with a plausible solution and called the Queen to inform her of the plan.

The Queen in turn went to find Roland to break the bad news. 'There has been such a bad accident,' she told him. Roland looked at her expectantly with a slight gleam in his eye. 'Your servant has been hurt.'

The gleam in Roland's eye disappeared.

'He is unconscious at the moment but we think what happened was that he found a dagger in his possession, knew that Palace rules forbade any weapons, and was on his way to take it to the armoury. Unfortunately James, not realising that anyone else would be using the stairs, had carelessly left some chairs on the landing and your servant has stumbled over them in the dark, fallen down the stairs, causing the dagger to fall into his leg. The doctor is with him as we speak. The doctor also has brought a nurse from the village. It is a most regrettable incident and we will cancel our small party if you believe it would be better.'

Roland recovered his composure and said he could not disappoint the ladies, so he believed the party should continue. He asked if he could visit his servant to see what he could do to assist, but he begged the Queen to continue with her plans and he would join the party as soon as he could.

'Of course,' said the Queen. 'If you have any request for anything which you believe would help in the recovery of your servant, you have only to ask and it will be done immediately.' The Queen fussed over him with many expressions of concern and regret. She tried hard to be sincere but in her heart she was exceedingly angry.

Roland found the doctor attending to his servant surrounded by bowls of hot water, bandages and several lethal-looking instruments set out on a table. A respectable looking lady was hovering in the background.

'Ah,' said the doctor, 'come in, come in. I understand you will be anxious, but I must warn you that you may not want to watch this.' The doctor proceeded regardless. 'You will note that I have removed the, er, problem and have cleaned the wound. I am going to stitch it now while he is still unconscious. It's better for him and, as it happens, much easier for me.'

The doctor had found that explaining details of his

methods and the care to be taken improved the patient's chances of recovery.

'Will you be blood-letting?' asked Roland, anxious to leave if that should be the case.

'I think this poor man has lost enough blood as it is, judging by the puddle. Ah, sorry.' The doctor noticed Roland had gone white. 'I'm not too sure about the efficacy of blood-letting. I have had some success with very large people when their heart rates are high, but I nearly lost a young patient once using the technique. I saved her with lots of saline draughts but it took a long time for her to recover. So I hesitate to use it now. What I need to do now is to stop the bleeding and keep the wound clean. With careful nursing and good food he should recover well. I will leave medication to help should he wake in pain. This good lady is experienced in these matters and will take good care of your servant.'

Roland asked if the lady would inform him immediately if the man regained consciousness. He now had to concentrate on an appearance of normality.

The party was a success. James thought Gabriella looked tired and pale. He put it down to the loss of her father but was also worried if her night-time expedition had harmed her at all.

'Not at all, James,' Gabriella told him. 'Please do not worry. It is taking a little time for me to recover from my father's demise and I have one or two small matters I need to attend to since it happened. I am sure everything will work out well. What do you think of my shawl? I am still setting a good example by dressing in a simple style, you'll note, but I believe I need to liven things up a little.' Gabriella had taken an old silk scarf which Florence had thrown out, washed it and darned the holes prettily. Gabriella did not realise it, but the cream colour set off her dark hair beautifully.

'I do not think it would be good for your character to tell you,' said James. 'Nanny says we must be modest. Would you do me the honour, young lady, of dancing this country reel with me?'

The other young ladies found James to be absent minded; his thoughts were often elsewhere and his answers to their questions did not always make sense. Roland, however, was the life of the party and danced with as many of the young ladies as he could.

Chapter Eleven

The next morning Roland was up early, having been called by the nurse so say that his servant had awakened and, apart from being in pain, was in reasonable health and she hoped for a full recovery in time. Roland told her to take some breakfast and he would attend the patient while she was away.

Roland was pleased to see that his servant's wound was hidden beneath blankets. His face was pale but Roland could cope with that. 'Well, Biggs, you made a real mess of that, didn't you,' Roland said in a whisper. He was irritable after lack of sleep and worry.

'You and your plans,' began Biggs. But Biggs's biggest worry was that he would be charged with a crime. He might be faced with having to spend the rest of his life in the guardhouse. 'Just keep me out of jail.'

'Keep your voice down,' urged Roland. 'Here's the story. You were looking for the armoury to leave the dagger, when you got lost. After the attack on the Prince, you were naturally alert and the noise you heard on the staircase made you think someone was waiting to cause more harm. So you crept down the stairs to see if you could prevent any more attacks on the Prince. You are naturally pleased that there was no danger and that you were the one to be hurt, not the Prince.'

Biggs did not like the last bit but Roland told him he must accept the story and convince the nurse, at least, of its truthfulness. 'It will keep you out of jail, so make sure you put on a good show.'

After breakfast that morning the King sent for James and the Captain of the Guard to discuss the progress in the investigation.

'My officer, young Smithick, found the trail without any difficulty,' said the Captain. 'But there was nothing along the way, and nothing had been dropped, to indicate who had made off with the Prince. Once Smithick got to where Prince James had been chained to a tree, he found a set of tracks leading down to the lake where they disappeared. He thinks that Mr. Gilbert had someone to help him rescue the Prince.'

'Yes, he did,' said the King. 'I know all about that.'

'Would it help our investigations to know who it was?' asked the Captain looking at James.

'No, not at present,' said James.

'Very well. My other men had little success with the locals in the area of the capture. An inn keeper says three strangers bought ale that afternoon and appeared to be arguing about something but he could not say what. He gave a description of them and it is obvious they were our visiting nobleman and his two servants. The two servants left Sir Roland at the inn for about two hours while Sir Roland had his dinner and when they returned they all left, after asking directions to the Palace. There were some sightings of three men riding along the road towards the Palace but that would be consistent with them travelling here.'

'Did anyone see what the two servants were doing for the hours they were missing?' asked the King.

'One small boy said he saw them riding in the forest, but we were not sure what conclusion we could place on that information, or if it was reliable. However, I must admit to distrusting the two servants, especially given the incident on the stairwell. It is possible that the servant was hoping to, um, hurt the Prince and then ride off quickly before anyone knew what had happened. His horse was saddled and waiting in the stable yard, so I do have grave suspicions.'

'To say nothing of Roland,' said the King.

'Yes, I did not like to say so, of course, but . . .' The Captain shrugged his shoulders.

'We need to have definite proof,' said the King. 'I cannot accuse Roland of anything without it or I will cause serious trouble. He came to me this morning with a farrago of nonsense but I cannot prove his story to be false at present.'

'I'd like to do a little investigation of my own, considering it's my life at risk,' said James. He outlined his plan.

'I don't want you doing anything dangerous,' said the King. 'Why can't you let the Guard do this?'

'As you can imagine, Sir, I am intensely interested in finding out for myself what danger I am in. What I intend to do is not expected by Roland or his men, so there would be no danger at all.'

'I don't like it,' said the King, 'but we have little else to go on as yet. But you must take at least two others with you.'

'Smithick would be a help, if you can spare him, Captain,' said James. 'And I have one other in mind but I will have to ask first.'

* * *

It was a relief to everyone at the Palace when Roland took his departure. His servant had not recovered quickly and was walking with a cane. Roland hired a small carriage to carry him home. This would make their journey much longer and Roland got extremely angry about it. But in private the servants had told him that if he left them in Essenia they would tell the King everything they knew, however much money Roland gave them. Roland gave in.

Two hours after Roland's departure the young officer, Smithick, entered the Palace grounds by a back gate dressed in old clothes he had been given by Mr. Gilbert. They smelled strongly of the stables. He was met by James.

'Good morning, Sir,' said Smithick in surprise.

James was wearing an old riding jacket which was too tight for him and the sleeves ended halfway up his arms, but it was all William Gilbert could find. An old pair of riding breeches and a large floppy hat with a wide brim completed the outfit. James hoped the hat would hide most of his face but he combed his hair forwards over his brow. He could pull an old scarf over his mouth when they left.

'You had better call me Jim,' said James, 'or you might call me Sir by mistake at the wrong moment.'

'Yes, er, Jim. You can call me Sam, Sir, sorry, Jim.'

They rode out of the Palace's back gate to the back of James's uncle's place of business where they found Peter about to mount his horse. He nearly fell off when he saw James.

'Wherever did you get those clothes?' asked Peter. 'Are you looking for the maiden who will love thee for thine own self and not for thy money?'

'I've already found her, thanks. And everyone knows I have no money,' said James.

'That's true,' Peter sighed. 'Why can't I wear something like that? I always wear this stuff.'

James laughed. 'You have to look like the merchant you are. We need to get moving, so come on.'

Companionably, they rode along the road to Grelland, and as evening approached they caught up with Roland at a wayside inn. Peter entered the inn by the front door while James and Sam took the horses to the stables. When James was sure no-one was about, he found where Roland's horses had been stabled.

'We'll find out where the two servants are eating and we'll try to sit near them,' said James quietly.

'I can stay in the stables in case they come out, if you wish,' said Sam.

'No, I want you to eat something. They won't be out here until very late. But before they do come out, we'll get you up in that hayloft above their horses.'

They entered a back door to a crowded room and saw Roland's servants eating at a table beside the fire. James asked the barmaid for two meals and went to stand in front of the fire with Sam until a nearby table became vacant.

The barmaid came over. 'Is that your master in the front room? Cook asks if you'd take in his tray. We're awful busy and I can't leave the bar.'

James was about to say he would be delighted when he remembered his role. 'Or right, miss. But I want a extra bit o' pie for doing it.'

Sam choked on a mouthful of ale.

'You'll be lucky,' said the barmaid.

James took the tray into the front room to Peter who was at the next table to Roland. 'I hope everything is to your liking, Sir?' said James.

'Well now, let me see.' Peter looked at his tray critically. James nudged the glass of ale on the table but Peter saw what he was doing and caught it.

'You are clumsy, Billings,' said Peter. James pulled a face under his hat but went back to his own dinner to find an extra piece of pie on his plate.

When Roland had finished his dinner, Peter signalled to the barmaid and asked her to call his servant. James came in quickly. 'I think it's time,' whispered Peter.

James went back to Sam and they left by the back door. James helped Sam get into the hayloft before going back to the inn to keep an eye on Roland's two servants. It was not long before the servants drained their tankards and went out the back door.

James waited a few moments before following them out.

He had to wait in the darkness by the door until he was sure they had entered the stable, before quietly hiding behind the wall at the back of the stable.

When Roland left the dining room, Peter also waited for a minute before following him out, this time by the front door of the inn. No-one else was out there on that cold night. It was quiet so Peter could hear Roland walk across the stable yard at the back of the inn and there was a short flash of light from the servants' lantern as he entered the stable. Peter silently took his place at the other end of the stable to James. Both were ready to help Sam if anything went wrong.

Roland was waiting for his men who had come out to see to the horses.

'Were you followed out here?' asked Roland.

'No, and no-one has followed us since we left the Palace.'

'Now, look,' said Roland, 'so far you've made a mess of things and next time I need things to be done properly.'

'We're not so sure there'll be a next time,' said one of the men. 'So far you've not given us enough money to make it worth our while putting ourselves in danger. Look what's happened to Biggs here.'

'It's his own fault,' Roland's voice was raised.

'Hush,' said Biggs. 'We don't want everyone in the inn to wonder what's happening. Your plans are the problem.'

'Look, there's nothing I can do now until next July. All the time I've been in Essenia I've been followed by a couple of guardsmen and I'll not get another invitation to the Palace before July. I've already been invited to the ball, so the Palace can't refuse me now. After that I'll be so rich you won't have to worry about money.'

'We'd like to see some of it now.'

'You've had enough. Look, if you want the money you'll have to earn it. Tomorrow morning I'm riding on ahead of you, so listen carefully.'

The two men fidgeted about but told Roland to go on and they'd see.

'I can't do anything until the ball in July, and anyway, I've got a lot of other plans to make before then. At the ball I'll want you to capture the Prince. It should not be difficult with so many people around. I'll get him to go outside the ballroom somehow. Then you take him a long way away and this time we'll make sure he's done in before you leave him. I'll make foolproof plans before then. In the meantime you'll need to change what you look like. Your appearance is far too scruffy. Grow moustaches or something. I'll get one of the military staff to teach you how to polish your shoes and keep your clothes clean. If you don't, the Essenian Guard will immediately suspect you and you won't get the opportunity to get hold of James. Don't contact me until I send for you.'

Roland left them and walked back to the inn. Peter edged further back into the shadows. Both he and James had to wait for Roland's men to rub the horses down and go back into the inn before they could be sure it would be safe for Sam to leave the hayloft.

Once Sam was safely down, he asked James if he had heard anything.

'Not much, it was too muffled.'

'It's not good, Sir, not at all.' Sam told him what he had heard. 'Can we arrest them the minute they come back to Essenia?'

'I think we are going to have to catch them red-handed. I'm just as worried about what else Roland is planning to do before July. If Roland comes back to Essenia I'll ask the King to have him followed to see what he is up to.'

Peter said he didn't like the whole thing. He'd never heard anything so dastardly, but he was willing to help anytime. 'Whatever is going to happen to make Roland so rich after the ball?'

'I have no idea but we have time to find out and make

plans,' said James. 'It's important now to make sure Roland doesn't find out who we are. Are you up to riding back to an inn closer to home? We'll have to leave quietly.'

They led the horses out of the stables as quietly as possible and walked down the road for a distance before mounting.

'How did you know?' asked Peter

'Know what?' asked James.

'That they wouldn't talk about what they were going to do until they stopped for the night.'

'I took a chance, of course, but it seemed to me that they would not be able to talk until later. One of the servants was in the carriage. Roland and the other servant were unlikely to discuss anything without him. And it's not so easy to talk when you are riding. They couldn't talk anywhere at the Palace because the King had ordered two of the guardsmen to follow them closely. So the only opportunity they would get to talk was at the end of the day after they had eaten. Roland wouldn't eat with his men so it had to be in the stables afterwards. It was just fortunate that, because they were near the Grelland border, Roland had decided to leave his men the next day to make their own way home.

'And, by the way' asked James, 'who is Billings?'

'Our newest office boy,' said Peter. 'He's always knocking something over. His name came to mind for some reason.'

Chapter Twelve

On a cool morning in early spring Gabriella answered the door to a stranger.

'I would like to speak with Mrs. Valencie, if you please,' said the gentleman.

Gabriella showed him into the library and told him she would see if Mrs. Valencie was available.

'What did he look like?' asked Mrs. Valencie, when informed of the visitor.

'Just an ordinary gentleman.'

'Is he fat?'

'He might be, but it's not a warm day and he's wrapped up with a thick coat and scarf.'

'If he's who I think he is, tell him I am out.'

'I suspect he would know that is not the truth because if that were the case I would have told him so immediately. And it would be quite difficult for me to know if he is the man you are thinking of.'

'Well tell him I am not well or something. Just get rid of him.'

'I'll try.'

Gabriella went back to the library and informed the gentleman that she was very sorry but Mrs. Valencie was not receiving visitors today.

The man's face turned red and he replied as if holding his anger at bay. 'Perhaps you would be kind enough to inform

Mrs. Valencie that I cannot come on another day, that I have travelled a long distance to see her and it is imperative that she sees me immediately. I can wait for a short time only.'

Gabriella climbed the stairs again and told Mrs. Valencie that her visitor was not going not go away until she saw him.

Mrs. Valencie became agitated. 'Go and get me an onion and a knife from the kitchen, girl, and be quick about it.'

Gabriella looked at her in surprise but left the room as ordered while Mrs. Valencie grabbed a pot of white powder and started to puff it on her face.

Once supplied with the onion, Mrs. Valencie cut it up until tears streamed down her face. By the time she had finished she looked ill. She had to reapply some powder but with a handkerchief to her nose, she appeared to be coping with a heavy cold.

'Go back to the kitchen, Gabriella,' said Mrs. Valencie. 'I will show him out myself.'

Gabriella did as she was bid and returned to wash the breakfast dishes. She told Nanny of the odd visitor. 'I think my step-mother wants me out of the way so that I don't overhear anything.'

Nanny said she would take a bucket of coal up to the drawing room and make sure nothing was wrong in the library.

'I am a little worried, Gabriella,' said Nanny on her return. 'That man is shouting at Mrs. Valencie and she is trying to make him keep his voice down. I couldn't make out what they were saying, not that I would listen, of course.'

'I can't do anything about it, Nanny. I was told to stay here. But I'll go up shortly if we think it's going on for too long.'

However, soon after that they heard the front door bang and Mrs. Valencie stamp up the stairs.

Gabriella heard no more about the incident. But the next morning Mrs. Valencie called her to her room.

'Now, Gabriella,' Mrs. Valencie began with a honeyed voice, 'I would like you to go to the market and look for some evening gloves for the girls. I am too busy with organising dresses for them. Here is some money and there should be enough for you to take a little refreshment in the tearoom after your shopping. There is no need to hurry.'

Gabriella went to look for Nanny and found her in the garden gathering herbs. She told her about the outing.

'Nanny, this is most unusual and I am feeling a little anxious. I have no idea what my step-mother is up to, but I'm certain she wants me out of the way. I wonder if you would be able to keep an eye on what she is doing. Would you have time to take some things upstairs occasionally? Don't do anything that would get you into trouble.'

'I know what I'll do, Gabriella. I'll get Mr. Georges in here to make some noise. He can stoke up the fire or stir the pots while I find out what is going on. Don't worry. I can do it without Mrs. Valencie knowing. Off you go and take advantage of the little free time you have.'

Gabriella came back just before lunch. There was no time for Nanny to tell Gabriella the news until lunch had been served.

While she ladled soup into bowls, Gabriella told Mrs. Valencie that she had bought the gloves as instructed. 'I saw some ribbons which Matilda and Florence may like, but I didn't buy them because I was unsure if they were the best colour.'

Matilda was interested and asked what colour they were. 'I need some red ones,' she said.

There followed a heated discussion between Mrs. Valencie and Matilda as to whether red was the right colour, so lunch passed in its usual noisy way until the ladies went into the drawing room and Gabriella went to clean the dining room.

So it was some time before Nanny was able to take

Gabriella out into the garden. 'We won't be disturbed here,' she said.

'Did you manage to find out if anything happened, Nanny?'

'I had no problem at all, child. The girls were arguing about who was to wear that cream shawl of yours if they got invited to the Palace again, so I was able to creep upstairs without being heard. But Mrs. Valencie was in your room, Gabriella. I was so angry that I nearly went into the room to find out what she was doing there. But I thought it might get you into trouble, so I just listened at the door. She was muttering something about where could they be, or where were they, or something like that. She was going through your cupboards and drawers. You had better go up there in a minute and see if anything has been taken.'

'There is nothing up there she could want, Nanny. My step-mother took all my good clothes and shared them between the girls. I did say I would not need them anymore so I suppose she thought I would not mind. Is that all she did?'

'Well, not quite. I had to stay in the kitchen for a while when I realised she was finished in your room. Then she came downstairs and went into the library and started rooting about in your father's desk, as far as I could hear.'

'That's odd. Whatever is she looking for?'

'I'm not sure, Gabriella.'

Chapter Thirteen

James often thought of the events of that winter. One of the more puzzling matters was that of Gabriella. James's experience with young ladies was that they were easily tired, did very little and preferred to sit rather than be active. How it was that Gabriella had been able to row a boat over a long distance was perplexing. James decided to experiment.

A young relative of the Queen was visiting from Farren. Jemima, a very cheerful young lady, had come specifically to visit the Queen, so James was not required to entertain her. However, the Queen decided a picnic in Jemima's honour would be appropriate.

Spring was well under way and the warmth was perfect for an outing. Several of the local young people were to attend. James warned them not to wear their best clothes as there would be some games on the small beach beside the lake.

The young men came in their sporting clothes but the young ladies found it hard to appear at an outing with the Prince unless they had on their newest gowns. Gabriella had declined to attend but Matilda and Florence came in particularly unwieldy dresses. They both tried and failed to look decorous sitting on the blankets provided by the Queen's kitchen maid.

Jemima, however, was dressed far more suitably. Matilda thought Jemima looked very odd in her short-sleeved blouse. She noticed that Jemima's skirt had no hoop and was not long enough to cover her ankles. Jemima, however, was there to enjoy herself. She played badminton with Peter, who had been given an afternoon off to attend. He only just managed to keep up with her. Then they both played bowls with some of the other young ones.

James looked around him and wondered which young lady would be able to row across the lake in freezing temperatures in the dark. He decided none of them would. But he was determined to get to the bottom of the problem so invited one or two to take a short trip in the rowing boat. Two ladies agreed. One brought her parasol with her. They both took a long time to get into the boat due to their cumbersome gowns but once in the boat, James shoved off and rowed them gently around close to the shore.

'Would either of you like to try rowing?' he asked. But neither thought it a good idea. They said they might upset the boat or get their gowns dirty. He took them safely back to the jetty and asked Jemima if she would like to try. Peter asked if he could come too and the three of them set off.

Jemima sportingly attempted to row. She said she had never done it before but it couldn't be too difficult. She grabbed the oars, stuck them in the water and pulled hard.

'Not so deep,' said James, laughing as she pulled in vain.

'Right,' said Jemima. She got the first pull about right and tried again. Sometimes the oars were too deep and sometimes they were a little shallow.

'I've had a bath, thank you,' said Peter as he dodged the spray.

James whispered to him. 'Just wait. She'll be in the bows with you in a minute.'

'I heard that,' said Jemima as she took a particularly shallow pull, and she did indeed land on Peter's feet.

Laughing, they soon pulled into land in time for some afternoon tea. Jemima said it had been good fun but her arms were aching.

James thought he was no further forward in his quest for an answer to Gabriella's actions. Some of the young ones were invited to stay for supper and James was able to ask Peter if he thought there were any ladies who would be able to row all the way across the lake.

Peter said his mother's housemaids might be able to do it.

'Last year, one of the housemaids got chicken pox and for two weeks I had to carry water up the stairs. My muscles ached for days. But the maids had never complained before. After that my mother altered one of the rooms downstairs to include a bath so that the water only had to be carried from the kitchen to there. But the maids still carry buckets of coal to the rooms above. As for the daughters of gentlemen, most of them would have trouble just walking the same distance as across the lake.

'It's a bit of a problem for me,' Peter told James. 'My father won't allow me to marry anyone but a gentleman's daughter. But I do not have enough money to support a lady of leisure. My wife will have to do something in the house unless she has plenty of money, but there are very few like that in Essenia.'

'What about Jemima?' asked James.

'I like her a lot, don't you? But I don't know her circumstances well enough and I'm worried I might get fond of her and then find I can't ask her to marry me. Although,' Peter added,' it might be a bit late already.'

'I'll ask the Queen, if you like,' said James.

'Do it discreetly then,' said Peter laughing.

James thought about the conversation and started to worry about Gabriella. What was she doing to be fit enough to row a boat across the lake?

Chapter Fourteen

Mr. Browning, the solicitor, had received some statements concerning his clients' accounts. He noted that one bearing Mrs. Valenice's name had made a small gain. Two others had made significant gains and Mr. Browning smiled to himself. He put these last two reports into his strong box and locked it securely with two keys for the simple reason that they bore Miss Gabriella Valencie's name.

Mr. Browning decided to send John once more to Derville with instructions to make enquiries at various inns, boarding houses and even the workhouse, and to do it attracting as little attention as possible.

'You may have to offer some money for the information so I am giving you this purse, but I'd be grateful if you would use as little as possible. And don't get drunk.'

John grinned. 'Of course not, sir. You know I don't drink. You can rely on me.'

'You are a good man, I know, John. Do your best.'

* * *

The King called James to him one evening in late spring.

'I have been thinking about Miss Gabriella,' said the King. 'We have done nothing for the young lady to show our appreciation. What she did was outstanding and I find it hard to understand why she does not want anyone to know. There must be more to it than modesty. We gave our head groom a present of money but I do not believe it would be correct to give Miss Gabriella the same. The Queen and I would like you to think of something which would be appropriate to help the girl in some way.'

'Yes, I have wondered myself what to do,' said James. 'But although we spent much time together when young, I have not been able to find out exactly what Gabriella's life is like since her father died. If you would allow me to take a few days to find out maybe I can give you a solution.'

'Of course, dear boy, take whatever time you need. You know you do not have to work as hard as you do.'

James went to the Queen and asked her if she would be able to invite Mrs. Valencie and her two daughters to afternoon tea sometime.

'Oh dear, James,' said the Queen. 'I do find it hard to know what to talk about with her. I will ask one or two others as well and perhaps Mrs. Rodriguez will come too. Do you want me to invite Gabriella? It might look odd if I don't.'

'No,' said James. 'Not this time, if you please. I have a little something in mind I need to do. It is unlikely Gabriella will come even if invited but I need to make sure she does not.'

'As you wish,' said the Queen. 'Now what cakes can I bake?'

The following Thursday afternoon, Mrs. Rodriguez came early to the Palace and gave the Queen a basket. Inside the Queen found a large cream cake and some tins full of biscuits.

'Just a few things to help with your visitors, my dear,' said Mrs Rodriguez. 'I know how busy you are.'

Mrs. Valencie and her daughters arrived at the Palace wreathed in smiles. They were disappointed to find that the Prince was not there but found out he was expected later. Mrs. Valencie resolved to stay for as long as possible until he arrived.

Meanwhile James had waited near the stables until he

saw Mrs. Valencie climb the steps to the Palace, and then he set off the way she had come. It only took him a few minutes to reach Mrs. Valencie's house. Mr. Georges opened the door to him but apologised, saying that the ladies had gone out for the afternoon.

'I know,' said James. 'I mean, I wonder if Miss Gabriella is here.'

'She may be a little busy at the moment, but I can find out for you. Please go into the drawing room.'

James waited for some time and then Nanny entered the room with a tray of tea and biscuits.

'I'm sorry to have kept you waiting, Sir. Miss Gabriella sends her apologies but asks if you would excuse her today.'

'Nanny,' said James. 'Please tell me what is going on. What has happened since Gabriella's father died?'

'Oh Sir, I do not know what to say. Miss Gabriella will be upset if I say anything, but I must tell you that I am so worried. She is doing all my work for me. The reason she cannot see you now is that she is chopping sticks for the fire and has on a very old dress.'

'Nanny,' said James firmly, 'we'll take this tray of tea out to Gabriella and I will see for myself what she is doing.'

'I must admit, Sir, I would be most glad if someone could help her but I am so worried she will get into trouble with her step-mother.'

'There will be no trouble,' said James. 'Come along.'

Thus Gabriella soon found herself sitting on an old bench in the kitchen garden drinking tea with James. James noticed her old clothes and her dirty fingernails. She told James that if she told him what was happening he was not to mention it to anyone else at all. He promised not to do so although he had reservations about it.

So Gabrielle told him the story. 'I know my father was not a gambler,' said Gabriella at length, 'but who would believe me? But James, even Nanny does not know why

I really do this. If she knew, she and Mr. Georges would leave and they would be destitute. I cannot allow that to happen.'

James felt his heart sink. There was no easy answer to Gabriella's problem.

'It's blackmail, Gabriella. How did your father come to marry your step-mother?'

'My father's business took him to Grelland occasionally and he was invited to a colleague's house for dinner. My future step-mother was one of the guests. She had been widowed like my father. I believe they met on several other occasions. I suppose my father, who had been very happy with my mother, thought it would be a good idea to marry again. He told me he thought it would be company for me when he was away, especially as she had two young daughters about my age.'

'I expect he thought you were turning into a hoyden, roaming about the countryside with me and Peter,' said James.

'More than likely,' laughed Gabriella. 'James, please do not worry. One day something will happen and things will change, but for the moment all I can do is continue as I am.'

James took her grubby little hand in his and kissed it. 'We must make something happen,' he said.

* * *

Two days later in the early morning, a young lad in work clothes turned up at Mrs. Valencie's back door and asked for Mr. Georges.

'I've been told by the King's Secretary to come here to learn how to do the gardening,' he said. 'I'm to be a sort of apprentice.'

Mr. Georges looked him over. 'I've not heard anything about this. Are you sure the King sent you?' he asked.

'I got a letter,' he said importantly. 'I got to work in the garden and learn everything. When I done all that, I got to chop up sticks and things. I got my own dinner what the Queen give me. And she sent these for you.' He held up several brown packets of seeds.

Mr. Georges took the letter and spent a few minutes reading it. The boy got restless and played with a cat which had jumped into the back garden.

'Very well,' said Mr. Georges at length. 'You've come at a good time. There's plenty to do. First of all I must get the stove ready for the ladies to do the cooking.'

'I can do that,' said the lad. 'I'll have that done in a jiffy. You just show me where the stuff is and I'll get to work. Then we can do something with those seeds.'

'Indeed,' said Mr. Georges.

There was another knock on the door and, upon opening it, Mr. Georges found a stout girl holding out another letter to him. She asked for Nanny.

'Please, Sir, I'm to learn how to be a housemaid. The Queen said she didn't have time to teach me and would your missus do it. I'll do all the work when I know what to do. The Queen said she'd pay for me to learn.'

Nanny and Mr. Georges were somewhat bemused by the situation but Nanny told Mr. Georges to accept with good grace. She was certain the Prince was behind all this but she did not say so.

Gabriella, however, was determined not to accept this help. But she reckoned without Mrs. Valencie. It seemed that Mrs. Valencie thought she was doing the Palace a favour by accepting these young persons.

'I received a message yesterday from the Palace,' she told Gabriella, 'asking if I could help by way of training young people for their future in the King's service. There would be a small remuneration. I sent a message back to say I would be delighted to help. So while you do your work, you can train these young people at the same time.'

Gabriella left the room before she raised her eyes to heaven. She went to find the new recruits who were introduced to her as Susie and Bob.

Chapter Fifteen

One early summer morning, James was in the dining room eating a hard-boiled egg. He had given up trying to dip his toast into it but had found it tasted just as nice sliced up on a well-buttered piece of bread.

The Queen poured him a cup of tea.

'Jemima is a very nice person, isn't she,' said James.

'She is a lovely girl,' replied the Queen.

'Does she have any brothers or sisters?'

'She has an older brother, who looks after her and her mother. Her father died some years ago.'

'Oh, poor girl. Does she have any hobbies, such as, well maybe she plays a musical instrument or something? I don't really know what young ladies get up to.'

'I believe she can play the harp,' said the Queen. 'We must get her to play for us next time she comes, which I hope will be soon. Do you want to know anything else?'

James grinned. He decided to forget discretion. 'It's my friend Peter who wants to know. He really likes Jemima but unless he knows her situation he can't make her any offer. If he can't give her the life she is used to he will not make any offer at all.'

'Ah,' said the Queen. 'I can help you there. Her mother is elderly and the family has a little money but not a lot. Jemima runs her brother's household for him in the position of housekeeper. She also takes care of her mother who is ill at times. That is why Jemima came to visit. Her brother believed Jemima needed a break. His aunt came to visit so was able to keep his mother company for a while which left Jemima free to come to us.'

'That's not the easiest of situations for Peter. Jemima obviously is used to helping but it seems she is needed at home,' said James wistfully.

'These things have a way of working out, James. Besides which, I always thought that your uncle would eventually give Peter more responsibility in the business. In time Peter might even take it over, which means he would be in a position to help Jemima's mother by supplying more servants in the home.'

'Yes,' said James brightening. 'I hadn't thought of that.'

'James,' asked the Queen, 'are you sure you do not regret coming to the Palace? We cannot offer you much. We are delighted you are here and we have grown so fond of you, but we would always make other arrangements if you decided you did not want this life.'

'Not at all,' said James. 'This is my life now. I need to learn more but I am thinking about the country all the time. I have one or two ideas but I want to make sure they are feasible before I suggest anything.'

'What sort of things?' inquired the Queen.

'Education for one,' said James. 'In the area of agriculture, for instance, I believe we could improve our crop yield. And then there is the issue of housing and I need to think about how we will prevent flood damage in the future. There is so much to do but first of all we need some sort of income. I'm still working on it. These are all long term matters, of course. I do not expect to be able to solve problems immediately.'

'Excellent,' said the Queen. 'I will ask Mr. Secretary to make some inquiries on your behalf. He knows a great many people.'

'Thank you.'

'And James, are you disappointed that Jemima likes Peter?'

'Oh no.' James smiled. 'I have always thought that Gabriella and I would be together for life. But she seems so distant at the moment. I do not know how to go about finding out if she feels the same way. We hardly ever meet these days.'

James did not tell the Queen that while Nanny and Mr. Georges were alive Gabriella would never leave them.

'I understand Gabriella has been acting as housekeeper, although I have no idea why that is necessary,' said the Queen. 'But now she has extra help Gabriella should be able to spend a little time with us. Would you like me to invite her?'

'It would be difficult to invite her without her step-sisters and I find I cannot talk to Gabriella while they are around. But the last arrangement we had worked well. If you would be kind enough to invite Mrs. Valencie and her daughters again, maybe I can find time to visit Gabriella.'

The Queen rolled her eyes in mock horror. 'For your sake only would I put myself through that. Mrs. Rodriguez must come too.'

James laughed and said it was time he left. He had an appointment with the King's legal advisers to learn some of the rudiments of law.

* * *

Gabriella did indeed find a little time for herself. Now it was summer her room at the top of the house was warm enough to sleep in. She looked at her wardrobe and thought she might take the time to improve her clothes. She decided to alter some old dresses to suit more modern fashion. She took a dress down to Nanny to see what she thought.

'Miss Gabriella,' said Nanny. 'I have something to tell you. Come into my room and let me show you something.'

In Nanny's room there was an old chest which she opened

and showed the contents to Gabriella. There were lovely dresses, shawls, coats and various small items.

'When your mother died I packed all her clothes away waiting for you to grow up. Then your father remarried and I wanted to know the situation before I mentioned these clothes to the new Mrs. Valencie. I'm sorry to say it, Miss Gabriella, but I did not take to the new Mrs. Valencie, so I'm afraid I kept quiet about these things. I knew the new Mrs. Valencie would not enter my room, so the clothes have remained hidden for a long time. I think your father forgot about them.

'Then,' continued Nanny, 'when you insisted on working so hard I did not think it was time to tell you. You only wore old or very simple dresses, so I waited. The only problem we have now is that if you suddenly start to wear these clothes your step-mother will wonder where you got them from.'

'Oh Nanny, aren't they lovely? But you are right. I cannot suddenly appear in these. But it lifts my spirits to know I have them. We must think about it.'

* * *

The Queen issued her invitation to Mrs. Valencie for an afternoon when James was free. Once again James was able to slip away in the direction of Gabriella's home. This time he entered the house by the back door and found Gabriella seated in the sunshine darning a hole in a sheet.

He was content to sit and talk with Gabriella for the short time he could spare. His excuse for coming was to get a report on the progress of the two young persons who, in turn, had been summoned to the Palace to state what they had learned. James was pleased to see Gabriella's complexion had taken on a more rested look.

When it was time to leave he asked Gabriella which day she could go with him for a walk by the lake or a ride in the forest. 'I know you could only come if your step-mother was somewhere else but I might be able to arrange it.'

Gabriella was not sure. She knew in her heart that she wanted to go but where it was to lead to she did not know.

Nanny, when she heard of the matter, told Gabriella to go. 'Do not take things too seriously, dear,' she said. 'Go and we will deal with any consequences.'

'I would have to be disguised in some way. If someone I knew saw me with the Prince it would get back to my step-mother and I would be in trouble.'

Nanny could not think what the trouble would be but she said it was the ideal opportunity to wear one of her mother's dresses, and that Gabriella would have to try them on to see if they needed altering, either to fit her figure or to be more in keeping with what young ladies were wearing now.

The Queen objected to inviting Mrs. Valencie again so soon. 'She will come to expect it later on. We must think of something else,' she told James.

However Mrs. Valencie had found out that some new merchants were to visit the area soon and she had every intention of taking her daughters to look for cheap material to be made into dresses for them. Mrs. Rodriguez had discovered this plan and mentioned it to the Queen, who told James, who sent a message to Gabriella to be ready.

Nanny was delighted and when the time came she sent the new housemaid upstairs and the lad to the woodshed to chop kindling. She conducted Gabriella to the gate to meet the Prince. 'I should, by rights, come with you,' said Nanny. 'But if I do everyone will know who you are. As it is, lately you have only been seen in those simple dresses so no-one will guess it is you dressed like this. Take your mother's parasol with you. If you see anyone, you can hide behind it.'

* * *

James and Gabriella wandered along the shore of the lake. James steered the conversation away from any reminders of that dark night.

'Do you remember that time Peter took a pie from his mother's kitchen without asking? His father was so angry Peter was not allowed out for a week except with his governess.'

'And when my mother found out she said I should not have encouraged him and I would have to stay with Peter's governess too. Your uncle never did find out, did he?'

'No,' James laughed. 'But I came with you and Peter. The poor governess got fed up with it. She brought a book, didn't she, and let us play by the lake?'

'Yes, and told us that if we got our clothes wet we'd have to walk about for hours until they were dry. She wasn't going to allow us to get her into trouble.'

'So she did. Didn't we take off all our clothes just in case?'

'No, we did not!'

'Most of them, anyway.'

'Did you ever learn to swim, James?' Gabriella enquired.

'Yes, but not when you were around. Peter and I came to the lake sometimes in the evenings when it was quiet and no-one could see us. Considering we all spent a lot of time in boats it would have been a good thing if you had learnt to swim too, Gabriella.'

'Oh, I did.'

'You did?' James was surprised. 'How?'

'I watched the children from the town who came here to swim. The girls had nothing on except their vests. So I crept out of the house when Nanny was busy and practised until I could swim across the bay. Nanny found out, of course, from all the wet vests I put on the washing line. But she said she was happy about it because she did not have to worry so much about us playing in boats.'

Just then Gabriella noticed something moving in the trees edging the lake.

'James, who is that man hiding behind that bush?'

'Don't worry about him. I believe the King has asked the officers in the guard to keep watch over me. There are two of them who take it in turns to follow me whenever I am not in one of the departments in the city. Please do not look at him. He believes I don't know he is there. A few days ago I lost him accidentally. I had to retrace my steps and pretend I had dropped something until he found me again. I did not want him to get into trouble. You do not mind, do you?'

'Not at all' said Gabriella. 'It makes me believe you are safe. I wouldn't like to have to rescue you again.'

James put his arm around her. 'Come on,' he said. 'The Queen has given us a basket of food. We'll eat some of it, although she has given us enough for two days.'

* * *

One afternoon the Queen made a pot of tea, placed some biscuits, some with black edges, on a plate and took them to the study where she found the King and Mr. Secretary.

'Do you have a few moments?' she asked.

'Of course, my dear,' said the King. 'And you have brought us a very welcome cup of tea.'

'It's about James,' she said. 'He is so enthusiastic about trying to solve some of our country's problems that I wonder if we can help in any way. He has been so kind as to solve our succession difficulties that I feel duty-bound to help with his ideas. If we can make any of these plans succeed I would feel better about asking him to take on heavy responsibilities.'

The Queen explained some of James' proposals.

'As you know, Ma'am,' said the Secretary, 'most of our

income comes from agriculture. We are able to support ourselves to a great extent and there is a little to export. Mr. Valencie dealt in the wool industry so we need to find a replacement for his excellent services. Maybe I could look into that matter although I have been discussing it with James' uncle who would be willing to take it on now that Peter is showing such an excellent turn for business.'

'What we really need, Mr. Secretary,' said the King, 'is some natural resources. We do export timber but I think it is time we consulted the university as to any prospects in other areas. In the past we always muddled along satisfactorily but things have come to a head with the floods of last year.'

'We have a surplus of fruit this year,' said the Secretary doubtfully.

'Have we?' asked the Queen. 'Then we must make jam and sell it. It's is only a very small thing, though.'

'Every small thing adds up, and you never know what it will lead to,' said the Secretary.

At dinner that night the Queen was occupied with thoughts of jam making. 'What I need is someone who knows how to make jam. I have made some but I was not altogether satisfied with the results.'

'Nanny makes good jam,' said James.

'Nanny?'

'Mrs. Valencie's housekeeper.'

'Ah yes, of course. Is it better than mine?'

'Your jam is delicious,' said James diplomatically. 'It's wonderful on your scones with cream. I eat it with a spoon so as not to miss any.'

The Queen looked pleased.

'But,' said James, 'Nanny's jam manages to stay on the bread somehow. I do not know how she gets it to do that.'

'We must ask her,' said the Queen. 'What are you doing next Wednesday?'

'I'm working in the stables. I have to muck out and help build a compost heap for the gardener.'

'They can manage for the day without you,' pronounced the Queen.

Chapter Sixteen

The Queen sent Mrs. Valencie a letter. There were many flowery compliments which the Queen believed Mrs. Valencie expected, and then it continued:

'The Palace would be most grateful if you would allow us to avail of the services of your housekeeper for one day. We wish to consult her on some domestic arrangements. If you would be so kind as to allow her to visit us we will provide a replacement servant for the day. Your housekeeper may feel more comfortable if she is accompanied by Miss Gabriella Valencie, if Miss Gabriella would be willing to spend a day in our kitchens.

'In due course we will be arranging a small dinner party to which we will extend invitations to you and your daughters, if you are able to accept.'

The Queen finished the letter with a flourish and sent the kitchen maid to deliver it.

When Matilda heard of Gabriella's invitation she complained bitterly. 'Why is Gabriella asked to go? It would be far more fitting if I went.'

'Do you really want to spend the whole day in the kitchens?' asked Mrs, Valencie. 'The Prince will not be there. I have never heard of a prince in the kitchens.'

Matilda had not thought of this and the prospect of a long boring day lost its appeal.

The following Wednesday Nanny and Gabriella got into the carriage sent by the Palace. For the occasion, and because her step-mother would not catch sight of her, Gabriella was dressed once again in one of her mother's pretty silk dresses.

'It's not really suitable for the kitchen,' Gabriella had objected when Nanny laid it out for her.

'I don't think the Queen has any intention of you remaining in the kitchen,' retorted Nanny.

Jenny met them at the Palace door and conducted them to the kitchen where the Queen had displayed some jars of jam on the table. There was also a tray of coffee and cakes which the kitchen maid offered to the guests.

'Nanny,' said the Queen, 'I believe you are able to make jam and I would be most grateful if you would tell me where I am going wrong. But I do not believe it is necessary for Miss Gabriella to be troubled with these small matters, therefore I have arranged for James to take her for a walk about the gardens. She will find it far more interesting that sitting with us, if she wishes.'

Nanny said it would be far better for Gabriella to be out in the fresh air and she could take her time. Jam-making was a lengthy business. Jenny conducted Gabriella to the hall where James was waiting.

In the kitchen the Queen showed Nanny a pot of strawberry jam. 'I cannot get it to set,' she said. 'Look, I have to pour it on the scones. Now the marmalade is a very different story.'

The Queen gave Nanny an opened pot of marmalade. 'See if you can get any out,' said the Queen.

Nanny tried to stick a knife in it but the knife skidded across the surface. She tried again with no success. Nanny knew she was going to giggle and did her best to hide her face behind her hand.

'I know, Nanny,' said the Queen, who also was laughing by now. 'You should have seen the King's face when I gave him this pot for his breakfast toast.'

'Oh, I am so sorry,' said Nanny, as she mopped up tears of laughter with her handkerchief.

When they recovered Nanny explained the jam-making process and the difference between strawberries and oranges. They set to work with some blackcurrants.

Meanwhile James had escorted Gabriella to the walled garden where he thought she might like to sit for a while.

'Why is the Queen suddenly interested in making jam?' she asked.

'This is a highly secret matter concerning national security,' said James with his nose in the air.

'It is, is it? Then why do I know about it?'

'It was thought you could be trusted. The nation is about to become very rich by selling jam to other countries. We do not want anyone else to know about it or they might start the business themselves and ruin our profits.'

Gabriella chuckled. 'And how are you going to set about doing that?'

'Well, we are not sure the marmalade will sell well just yet, so we need to take the time to experiment and do extensive research.'

James did not find the mysteries of jam-making very interesting. 'We can't do anything about it until we have some funds to set up the industry. It's just one of the plans we have and I would like to make it work for the Queen's sake. She is doing this for me, in an effort to help me keep the country solvent. Would you like to see the view from the top of the hill?'

'I was going to suggest it,' said Gabriella, 'but I was worried you might not cope with the exertion. You appear to like sitting in the sun.'

James spluttered. 'Come on, young lady, I'll race you to the top.'

Chapter Seventeen

James and Gabriella walked along the ridge of the hill where mountains and valleys tumbled about before them all the way down to the sea. Gabriella took a deep breath of the fresh air wafting up from the ocean.

'Are you happy here, James?' she asked.

'Yes, more than I thought I would be. I took on the job thinking it was the right thing to do but with no prospect of enjoying it. I thought the responsibility would be too great.'

'And is it?'

'Not as much as I thought. I realised that the King will live for a long time yet so I have plenty of time to get used to the idea of ruling a country. Can you imagine how that felt coming from being the messenger in my uncle's business?'

Gabriella smiled. 'It's very different, of course. We might not have been so carefree as children if we had known what was in store for us.'

'It's a good thing we didn't know, especially your situation, which is far worse than mine. I wish I could do more for you.'

'Susie and Bob have made a big difference to my life, thank you. Before, I used to shudder every time I thought of what I had to do. I was trying to do the work of at least two people. The only way I survived was to take one minute at a time.'

James frowned. 'I wish I had known earlier.'

'Please do not worry. I couldn't say anything at the time

because Nanny would have found out. She and Mr. Georges would have left so that Mrs. Valencie would have to engage new servants and I would not have to do so much work. Nanny and Mr. Georges would not have survived for long without any income. But now there is no need for them to leave for my sake because we have Susie and Bob. Susie makes me laugh too, which is always a good thing.'

'Does she? I don't know her well but I can't imagine her being funny.'

'She tries so hard to help that things go wrong sometimes. The first time she cleared out the fire grate she attacked those ashes as fast as she could. When I went in to see how she was coping I couldn't see her. The room was full of dust. It got everywhere. I opened all the windows but it still took an hour for the air to clear. Susie thought she would get into trouble but I got a fit of the giggles and Nanny had to come and find out what we were laughing about. Fortunately my step-mother was out.'

'It seems to me she is causing you more work,' said James severely. 'What about Bob?'

'He likes the garden. The more mud he gets on his clothes and shoes, the happier he is. We had to teach him to take off his boots and shake his clothes before coming in for lunch. I like them both, James, and I am very glad to have them. But tell me, what are your plans for ruling the country? Are you going to have strict laws and make us slave for you, so you can amass great wealth? I'd like to know so I can prepare for the worst.'

'That's a good idea. Though I have no idea what I could get you all to slave at in order to make a lot of money. I suppose I could force everyone to make a lot of jam and sell it at exorbitant rates.'

Gabriella laughed. 'You'll have us up at the crack of dawn picking berries and pealing apples.'

'Definitely,' said James, grinning at the thought. 'Seriously though, can you see that field down there? The King gave it to me for my experiments. I discovered that some farmers in Farren grow different things in their fields each year and get better crops as a result. So I divided the field into four and got that young lad to plant different things in each segment. Next year we'll rotate the crops and see what happens. The gardener says he's been doing that for years. We need to experiment with unusual crops too. Then if we get good results we'll get farmers to change their ways. We'll have to start with young farmers who are willing to consider new ways. It's only a beginning, but if we can manage without importing a lot of food, we can turn our attention to other ways to generate income.'

The young lad in the field looked up and waved. James waved back.

'Oh, no, James,' said Gabriella. 'I can't be seen with you. It will get back to my step-mother. Can we go now?'

'Yes, of course. There are some people coming along the road in that carriage. I don't think they would recognise you though. The road is quite a long way down. Where is that umbrella thing you had?'

'My parasol? I left it in the garden. I didn't want to be bothered having to carry it up here.'

'Come on then. If we walk back down the hill we'll be out of sight in a few minutes.'

* * *

To further his plans, Roland travelled to the city near the Palace of Essenia and found himself some lodgings. It was not long before he noticed he was being followed discreetly. But this did not disturb Roland because he believed no-one could find fault with his activities at present.

This time his plans had to be foolproof. The debacle on the stairway at the Palace was unfortunate, but Roland believed he had managed to allay any suspicions of the truth on that occasion. His plans settled around the ball where there would a crush of people. This, he believed, would help him overcome the problem of how to get rid of the guardsmen who continually followed him. Somehow Roland needed to think of an excuse to get the Prince to go out of the back door of the ballroom where Roland's men could carry him away. But Roland needed to know the lie of the land better than he did, so that he could direct his men on the best road. Roland soon thought of a solution to the problem of how to do this without making the guardsmen suspicious.

Once settled in his lodgings, Roland got directions from a helpful servant to the home of Mrs. Valencie, and he presented himself there one morning.

Gabriella opened the door to him. She had her hair pinned back and was wearing a maid's apron so Roland did not recognise her.

'I wish to visit Miss Valencie, please.'

'Certainly, Sir, which one would you like to see?'

Roland had not paid attention when he had been introduced to Miss Matilda and Miss Florence at the Palace dinner party. It was his understanding, having read the genealogical records, that there was only one Miss Valencie, so he was at a loss for words for a while. He then realised that the genealogical records he had looked at must be out of date or incomplete.

'The eldest Miss Valencie, if you please.'

Gabriella opened the door wider. 'Certainly, do come in. If you would care to wait in the drawing room I will fetch her for you. Would you care for some tea?'

Roland said he would.

As it happened, Matilda was older than Gabriella by two months. Gabriella climbed the stairs to tell her of the visit before going to make the tea.

Matilda reacted excitedly. Very few young men called to

visit her specifically. Fortunately she was already dressed for a walk, so all she had to do was redress her hair and apply some rouge and powder. By the time she entered the drawing room Roland was on his second cup of tea. He recognised her immediately.

'Good morning, Sir. How kind of you to visit,' said Matilda.

'We met at the Palace dinner, of course,' said Roland, bowing slightly. His planned speech explaining that he was calling to make the acquaintance of one who was related to him had to be adapted. 'I was reviewing the family tree recently and realised that you and I are related, although somewhat distantly. We had no time at the dinner to go into such matters with so much entertainment to be enjoyed.'

'Are we really related? That is a surprise, but a very welcome one naturally.' Matilda smiled.

Roland pursued the conversation lightly. They were interrupted by Miss Florence who flew into the room to find out who had called. Then Mrs. Valencie entered and there was so much noise with everyone talking at once that Roland felt overwhelmed. But his charm got him through and eventually he made his goodbyes with a promise to take the young ladies out for a drive in his carriage on the next day. He believed he had made good progress.

The following day was fine and Mrs. Valencie was pleased to wave her two daughters off, knowing she had done all she could to make them look as attractive as possible. Actually, Gabriella had done most of the work. She dissuaded Florence from wearing a large hat with a long feather, saying it made her look old. She wiped off much of the rouge on Matilda's face, telling her she looked as if she had a high fever. With a sigh of relief, Gabriella went back to the kitchens to peel potatoes.

In high spirits the two young ladies chattered non-stop, until Roland drove into the park where the girls could wave regally to passing acquaintances. When the excitement calmed, Roland asked if they had visited the Palace again or if there was any news of the King and Queen.

'Yes, we visit the palace regularly and we are expecting another invitation soon,' said Matilda. 'The Queen likes to have young company for Prince James. He prefers us to some others, of course.'

'Naturally he would,' said Roland gallantly.

The girls giggled. Matilda mentioned that the Prince had been seen walking about accompanied by a young lady of good fortune. 'We are all wondering who she is. Apparently she was dressed in very expensive clothes.'

'I heard that she is a princess and that the King and Queen wish James to marry her,' said Florence.

'I don't think he wants to,' said Matilda. 'When we visit he makes a point of speaking with me, you know.'

'Does he?' asked Roland.

'Oh yes,' said Matilda airily, 'I believe Prince James particularly requests the Queen to invite us.'

Roland was somewhat worried about this statement. He wondered if James was considering marrying the eldest Miss Valencie himself. But then Roland thought back to the evening dinner party at the Palace and could not remember James spending much time with Miss Valencie. If Roland could remember properly he thought that James had spent quite a lot of time talking with a young lady who, although undoubtedly pretty, had been too quiet and dowdily dressed for Roland's liking.

They discussed at length who the princess could be and where she was from. It was her clothes that interested Matilda.

'Some say her clothes are made by the best seamstresses in Farren, but they could also be from Grelland. Do you know which emporiums would supply royalty?'

Roland said he knew of one or two but these places were for the most elite of society and he did not know of anyone who visited those places who would fit the description Miss Valencie had given him of the mystery princess. 'I suspect that the Princess must be from Farren. If you discover who she is I would be interested to know. Prince James is a distant cousin of mine and I would like to offer my felicitations if such are called for.'

'I expect we will know very soon,' said Florence. 'But I do not think Prince James is contemplating marriage yet. He is required to help entertain visitors, so I expect the Princess is simply someone who is visiting the Queen.'

Roland began to see that association with these two young ladies could be more profitable than he had hoped.

'What does James do with himself when you are not visiting?' he asked.

'He spends a lot of time learning matters of state. I believe he finds it very boring and would rather be with us.'

Roland wanted to ask what sort of schedule the Prince had but decided it would be better to leave that to another time, but he would try to find out who the lady was that James was walking out with. If James was thinking of marriage, Roland's plans were urgent. He drove the ladies home. He asked if he could drive the ladies out the next day if the weather was fine. His aim was to drive the ladies around the area so that he could get to know which roads would best for his servants to take in their escape. Miss Valencie would surely know the roads better than he, so she could direct him as if they were simply enjoying the air. No-one would guess his real motives.

After Roland left, the girls discussed at great length every minute of the morning's outing, trying to decide if Roland felt a preference for one of them. Matilda failed to take into account that, if Roland was related to Prince James, he could not possibly be related to her. Even if she had, it is unlikely she would have clarified the situation.

Mrs. Valencie was overjoyed at the latest turn of events. Roland must be considering marrying one of her daughters.

* * *

Mr. Browning's clerk soon reported to his employer that he had made some progress in Derville and had found a man who might be able to help the solicitor. Unfortunately the man had asked for a very large sum of money in exchange for the information and John did not believe he could give him that amount.

'I did not trust him, Mr. Browning. He was a very scruffy individual and I did not know if he really had any useful information to give us.'

'Yes, thank you, John. I suppose I had better go to Derville myself. If you tell me where I can find this individual I'll contact him myself. If I go tomorrow, will you be able to manage here?'

'Of course, sir.'

'Yes, I think you will. If Mrs. Valencie comes to visit you may show her this statement of her account. Tell her I have paid her household bills and will discuss them with her when I return. However, she may ask you for an advance from this account, or for a general increase in her monthly payments. You will say that you, personally, are not able to make such decisions and she would do better to speak to me about it. Under no circumstances whatsoever are you to give her any money, no matter what story she tells you.'

* * *

Roland continued to take Matilda and Florence out for rides in his carriage. He told them he thought they might get bored with the same route every day, so he would take them in a different direction each time, if they would inform him of the best roads to take.

On these occasions and if Mrs. Valencie was out as well, Gabriella took the opportunity to look at her mother's dresses to see if they needed altering. She would sit with Nanny, either in the garden on nice days or in the kitchen if it was dull. It gave Gabriella a chance to talk about her mother with Nanny.

'Now this dress,' Nanny said, holding up one of cream muslin, 'your mother wore to a garden party at the palace. It's cool for the summer months. You were very young at the time and your mother would only go out for a few short hours until she came hurrying home to see if you were still asleep.'

Gabriella asked about the dress which she had worn the day she walked out with James.

'Your mother loved that dress. Your father had bought a perambulator which he had discovered on one of his business trips to Farren, so your mother was able to take you out in it nearly every day. Most times she wore that dress because her main aim in going out was to show you off to the neighbours. I offered to take you out for a walk but your mother always wanted to take you herself. It broke my heart that day when . . . but never mind that now.'

Nanny went to the chest to bring out something Gabriella had not seen yet. In her arms she had a gown of white silk. Nanny held it up for Gabriella to see.

'Nanny, it's wonderful. Do I have time to try it on?'

'We've plenty of time, child. Just make sure your hands are washed first.'

Gabriella shook off her apron and old dress and slipped into the dress Nanny held out to her. The bodice was tailored but had a ruche of gathered material hanging from the shoulders. The skirt was fitted at the waist but hung beautifully as it widened to her feet. A seamstress had sewn a border of white roses at the top of the bodice and had scattered a few also on the skirt.

'If we put your hair up, Gabriella, easily you would be

mistaken for a princess,' said Nanny as she surveyed the picture before her. 'Come and look at yourself in the mirror in my room.' Gabriella saw that Nanny was right but she was a modest girl and laughed at Nanny's admiration.

'I don't suppose I will ever have an opportunity to wear it,' said Gabriella.

'You'll wear it to the ball in July, surely,' said Nanny.

'I do not think my step-mother will allow me to go.'

Nanny got upset about this but tried not to show it. She planned there and then to find some way to make sure Gabriella went to the ball.

* * *

Mr. Browning travelled to Derville and after finding lodgings for the night went to the address his clerk had given him. This was a small inn down a back street in the poorer parts of the city. Mr. Browning could not find the individual John had mentioned but, after ordering a drink, talked to the landlord instead.

'I'm looking for a Joshua Sertus. Would you happen to know him?'

'I might,' said the landlord, quietly wiping glasses with an old cloth.

Mr. Browning laid a sovereign down on the bar.

'Well now,' said the landlord. 'I heard he had died.'

'Yes?'

'Mm, sad case it was, they said. He had a good business going and made some money but,' the landlord lowered his voice, 'he lost a lot to speculation.'

'What happened?' asked Mr. Browning.

'It seems it got to a point where he found he was in debt so much that he couldn't hope to pay it back, despite making good money. They say he ran away to sea and died in a storm.'

'And did he?'

'He might have done.'

Mr. Browning put another sovereign on the bar.

* * *

Roland was at a loss to know how to further his enquiries. He did not want anyone to think he was unduly interested in the doings of the Prince. He was still convinced that the only opportunity he would get to do away with James was at the ball. For the time being James was too well protected when he left the Palace. However Roland liked to keep an eye on what was going on, so he took the young ladies out driving when he could, or followed them to the lending library

It was just by chance Matilda discovered that Roland frequented the library. Her mother had sent her there one morning to return a book. Matilda had complained about having to go and asked her mother to send Gabriella instead. But Mrs. Valencie wanted Gabriella to show Susie how to clean the rooms.

'Susie does not dust properly,' she said.

So Matilda had insisted Florence keep her company so that they could visit the market afterwards. Matilda changed her plans once she saw Roland enter the library after her. She avidly browsed the shelves and exclaimed in surprise when he spoke to her.

'Good morning, Miss Valencie,' Roland said. 'What a lovely surprise to see you here. I did not know you were fond of reading.'

'Oh, yes,' said Matilda. 'I love to spend time with a good book. Florence is not so interested but I believe it is so good for one to consider the opinions of others.'

'Naturally,' said Roland, who had never heard Miss Valencie express interest in any opinions other than her own.

Florence joined them. 'I find the books available here so

limited. There really is no scope for education. Which books do you read, sir?'

'Novels,' said Roland in a spirit of mischief. 'There is a romance by a Mr. Gregory that I found quite exciting. And there is a possibility that Mr. Gregory may, in reality, be Mrs. Gregory.'

'Really?' said Florence. 'Is there a copy of it here today?'

'There may well be. I will look for you.' Roland found it easily and gave it to Florence.

'When you have read it, Florence, I will read it too,' said Matilda. 'It would be interesting to see if we can determine whether the author is a woman. I believe I would know by the style of writing. What sort of story is it?'

'It is about a princess who wishes to find her true love by pretending to be a peasant. She has many exciting adventures and has to be rescued by a rich young man who is also pretending to be a peasant. It gets quite complicated towards the end but I believe you will enjoy it.' Roland had only skimmed through the book but was confident neither girl would read it. The opening chapters described at great length the sadness of the princess who was so rich she only received offers from men who were interested in her wealth.

'Have you heard the latest story about the princess who visits the Queen at the Palace?' asked Matilda, abandoning her quest for culture.

'No,' he said but leant towards her conspiratorially.

'It is said that she and James are to be married soon, but I do not believe it.'

'Nor do I,' said Florence. 'He shows great interest in me when we see him. We are expecting an invitation to the ball soon and I am certain the Prince will make sure we get it.'

'Some say,' said Matilda, ignoring Florence, 'that the princess is very wealthy and that the King wishes James to marry her in order to help with the Palace finances. But I do not believe the Palace is short of funds. We are always given a very good meal when we dine there. However, if James is being forced into a marriage he does not care for, then I suppose he will put off the wedding as long as he can. Perhaps he hopes there will be some other way to make the King rich.'

Roland choked on something but recovered before Matilda sent Florence for a glass of water.

'It would be interesting to find out who this young lady, or princess, is,' said Roland. 'I wonder how we could find out.'

'I am not sure,' said Matilda. 'She was not at any of the parties we have attended at the Palace. We will probably have to wait until the ball. I would expect her to be present if the Queen wishes James to become betrothed to her."

'Nanny might know something,' said Florence.

'Would she?' asked Roland in surprise.

'She might have heard something when she was in the Palace kitchens the other day.'

'Does she often visit the royal kitchens?' asked Roland.

'No,' said Matilda quickly. 'She was required to help with some domestic arrangements. We are quite important to the running of the Palace, you know. We are training some staff for them just at present.'

Roland found this interesting. 'If we are to know who the princess is, we would need to know what the Prince is doing. Perhaps if you were to ask your Nanny discreetly of any news from the Palace we may find out.'

But Nanny told the girls sharply that she had only been in the kitchens and had discussed cookery with the Queen in order to help with her domestic arrangements. Nanny said she had not seen the Prince and she knew nothing about a princess. But the conversation worried Nanny a little. The Prince and Gabriella needed to be more discreet when they went for walks in future.

Chapter Eighteen

Roland's plan was to marry the eldest Miss Valencie as soon as possible. To this end he needed to get her on her own. His opportunity arose one morning at the library.

Florence had stayed in bed with a cold but Matilda was determined to go to the library and this time she insisted that Susie went with her. Matilda was not sure how Roland would react if Gabriella was present and she was not going to take any chances.

Roland greeted Matilda and passed the time of day with pleasantries. He discovered Florence was at home.

'Would you care for a cup of tea at the little tearoom nearby, Miss Valencie?' asked Roland. 'Your maid can go home as I will escort you home myself.'

Matilda became flustered but blurted out that she would be delighted. 'Just one moment, Sir, if you don't mind. I will give my maid instructions. She is a little simple.' Matilda dragged Susie outside the library and told her in, a hoarse whisper, to go home and tell no-one where her mistress had gone. Matilda said she would be home before lunch.

On the way to the tearoom, Roland took Matilda's hand and tucked it into his arm. 'May I call you Gabriella?' he asked.

Matilda was shocked into silence for a second but answered calmly enough. 'Of course, Sir, but please do not do so in my mother's hearing. She is a little strict.' Mrs.

Valencie was not particularly strict, and why Roland thought she was Gabriella, Matilda did not know but he could call her anything he liked. Thinking back, Matilda realised that she had never told Roland her name. Florence sometimes called her Sis which Roland would think was natural. Matilda planned to keep it that way.

Once in the tearoom Roland selected a quiet table and, after the tea had been served and drunk, asked Matilda for her hand in marriage. Matilda was thrilled and said yes promptly. Roland said he had a ring for her but would defer giving it to her until they had informed Mrs. Valencie of their plans.

'I would prefer to have your mother's blessing, Gabriella, and then I would be delighted if you would accept the ring.'

'Yes, certainly, Sir. Will we ask her when we get home?'

'Please call me Roland, in private, of course. But we will ask your mother without any delay.'

Roland's plans worked out well. He formally asked Mrs. Valencie for Miss Valencie's hand in marriage. It was granted with relief. In the days which followed Roland managed to avoid answering most of Mrs. Valencie's questions concerning Matilda's new life. He hoped that a small marriage ceremony could be arranged quickly. He planned to take his bride to live in his house in Grelland. They would certainly return for the ball in July but this would give Miss Valencie some time to adjust to her new way of life.

Matilda wanted a big wedding with several bridesmaids, flower girls and page boys, but here Mrs. Valencie put her foot down. 'I do not have the money for such a wedding, Matilda. Once you are married I expect you will have plenty of money for clothes and such like. But for now I will have to arrange something very simple. Roland has not offered to give me any money to help with the wedding. I will have to borrow some money as it is but maybe after your marriage Roland will help me with the debts. We will get Gabriella to do a lot of the work. She is good with flowers and dresses you nicely. Nanny can make a wedding breakfast.'

With that, Matilda had to be content. She dreamed of married life in which she would have plenty of money for lovely gowns and she would surely have a proper maid as befitted the wife of someone related to the King of Grelland. Roland had asked her if one of Mrs. Valencie's maids would accompany his bride to her new home. Matilda did not explain the exact nature of Mrs. Valencie's maids. She brushed off the question, stating vaguely that she would consider that detail later.

The only difficulty Matilda then had was how to keep her real name hidden during the wedding ceremony. Matilda did not know why it was so important that her name should be Gabriella but decided it would be better if Roland did not find out her real name until after they were married. Matilda could not see a problem with that. Once she was married it would not matter so much, but she was not going to take any risks beforehand.

Matilda took Susie with her to visit the minister who was to preside at her wedding. Leaving Susie at the entrance to the chapel, Matilda made discreet enquiries as to the vows.

The young minister was both inexperienced and kindly. He believed Matilda's questions stemmed from nerves. 'I have a copy of the usual vows,' he said, handing a sheet of paper to Matilda. 'Some can be changed to suit what the couple prefer to say but some of the vows are legal requirements.' He indicated which could be changed. 'I will need copies of your respective birth certificates too, so as to be able to fill out the necessary forms. It's best to get this done well in advance.'

It was not going to be easy, Matilda realised, but there was time to think about it.

Chapter Nineteen

Gabriella knew that lovely summer could not last. Susie and Bob would have to go soon or Mrs. Valencie would wonder why they remained after they had been trained. Sooner or later Gabriella would be back to doing a lot of hard work. But she was not one to dwell on those thoughts and decided to make the most of the time she had.

In June, James pleaded with the Queen to ask Mrs. Valencie and her daughters to a lunch. The Queen agreed.

'I might find it useful this time, dear James,' she said. 'They can help me with some decorations I plan to use in the ballroom. Mrs. Rodriguez can come too and help with conversation. If I tell them you will return to the Palace shortly, they will stay until you come, so you can take whatever time you need.'

Early the next morning James went to find Nanny in her kitchen before anyone else had risen. He asked her to tell Gabriella that he would be grateful if she would give him some time the next afternoon. James told Nanny the plan with regard to Mrs. Valencie and the girls.

'That's all very well, my dear, but your exploits are being talked about. Somehow people have seen you with Gabriella and they believe you are courting a princess.'

'Oh,' said James. 'Do you have any suggestions? It's very difficult for me to think of somewhere we can walk where we will not be seen. We do not have the time to drive a carriage to the coast or something like that. This outing is very important, Nanny.'

'Very well. Gabriella was going to the market tomorrow afternoon. She will be wearing her old dress. Do you have any old clothes so that we can disguise you this time? We could pretend you had been sent to help her carry the packages.'

'That may well work another time Nanny, but this occasion calls for good clothes. Can Gabriella go to the market another day? I will have to risk being seen this time and I think we will take our usual walk by the lake. I can take a different path. And do not worry about a chaperone. I know you would like to come with us and we would like your company but it would make us more conspicuous. As it happens, a guardsman or two follow me about everywhere after that episode the other night.'

'Well, I'm pleased to hear that.' Nanny believed she knew what the Prince had in mind for this outing, but she was uneasy about the whole thing. She simply told Gabriella that she was to walk out again with the Prince. She left out the information that it was something special. Nanny thought that Gabriella might not go if she guessed what was to happen.

So the next afternoon Gabriella met James at the gate in the pretty cream muslin dress her mother had worn to the garden party. The useful parasol was tucked under her arm.

As soon as they were walking beside the lake and James had made sure the guardsman who was following was at a distance, James presented Gabriella with a rose and, without preamble, asked her to marry him.

At first Gabriella was suffused with happiness. She wanted so much to say yes. But then she realised she could not marry James. Tears flowed down her cheeks.

'James, I am so sorry I cannot marry you.'

'Why not?' It was not the most romantic of questions but James didn't have time to waste. 'If you are worried about Nanny and Mr. Georges, then don't be. I explained a little of the situation to the Queen, who said she would be most grateful if Nanny and Mr. Georges would live at the Palace. She would have asked them before but she believed it was the same as stealing. She did not want to leave you without your old servants but I know she would welcome them if you came too. We would find them something to do. And they really would not have to do much. Actually thinking about it, we do not have a butler and it would be nice to have someone to answer the door, and Nanny could make jam in the kitchen whenever she wanted.'

Gabriella smiled through her tears. 'Thank you, James. That is a lovely thought. But I cannot rely on my step-mother not spreading rumours about my father. If Nanny left the house, my step mother would have to spend a lot of money replacing her and Mr. Georges. At present I do much of the work and do not get paid. I believe Mrs. Valencie would do something out of spite. All she has to do is mention quietly to someone, as if in confidence, that my father had lost all our money by gaming and the rumour would spread.'

'Why would she do such a thing?'

'There was a very strange man who came to our house the other day and since then he has called several times. Each time he comes, my step-mother gets into a terrible mood. Nanny and I are now guessing that she is in debt and needs a lot of money to pay it back. How she could have got into that state I do not know, but the solicitor says my father's affairs were not in such a good position as I thought. All my step-mother would have to say is that it was my father who had got her into debt.'

'But would it matter what she said if you were with me at the Palace?'

'It would distress me and would cast the Palace in a bad light. It's not only that, James. I need a dowry if I am to marry you and I have nothing at all, now that I know about my financial difficulties. I am ashamed to say it but that is the situation. I knew our friendship would have to end sometime. I should not have let it go so far but it was so pleasant to be with you I just put it off.'

'I am not the slightest bit interested in a dowry, Gabriella. We have nothing at the Palace either, so we know how to live with little. We have enough to eat and a roof over our heads, although it's leaking at present but I'll soon mend that. I cannot offer you much in the way of luxury, but you will have a home and will not need to work as you do now. Is that the problem, that I cannot offer you riches?'

'How can you think that, James? I need very little. But I do have this problem with my step-mother. On top of that, brides usually bring something to a marriage and I cannot. You must forget me now. Look around for someone else to marry. You will have to at some point, I expect.' The prospect filled Gabriella with grief.

'Who, for example?' asked James, with a grin.

For a moment Gabriella's frame of mind lightened. 'There was that girl at the Palace dinner who followed you around. She looked quite presentable.'

'You mean Violet March. Her head is full of little else but clothes and furnishings. She kept asking me who had on the prettiest dress and did I like hers. What could I say? I couldn't say no, I thought hers was ugly. I wanted to say that yours was the most beautiful but I could hardly say that without giving offence. Then she told me, in the sweetest terms, our ballroom was very pretty but it just needed new silk drapes and furniture from Farren to make it perfect. She'd have the country bankrupt in a month or two. I ran out of things to say to her after two minutes. You will have to do better than that.'

'Mm, maybe. So let me think. I can't really recommend my step-sisters.'

'No, don't. I would not like to be impolite.'

'What about that young lady who dashes about the town

in her carriage. She drives it faster than anyone would think possible. She might be fun.'

'She scares me to bits. I don't drive into town myself if I know she is on the road. Just imagine if I had to sit in the same carriage while she was driving? I'd die of a heart attack.'

'Yes, I suppose you might. If she is in the town when I go to the market I have to jump into a doorway to get out of her way. So now, let me consider. I've heard that a young lady from Farren visits the Queen. What is she like?'

'That's Jemima and yes, she is a lovely girl. But she likes Peter. Come to that, Peter likes her too and I believe he will ask her to marry him. I can't steal her from Peter. Besides which, she is not my type at all. I can't explain why, but you really are the only one there is.'

Gabriella was momentarily diverted. 'Is she really going to marry Peter? I would like to meet her? Would it be possible?'

'You'd like to see if she is the right person for Peter, I suppose.'

'Perhaps there is something in that. We can't forget our childhood friends even if we will not meet in future.'

'I can arrange for you to meet Jemima without any difficulty, but I'm not going to forget you or marry someone else. I will have to decline into a sad old man and pass on the kingship to someone else. Roland, I expect.'

Gabriella smiled again but sadly. 'No, really James, it's best if we don't meet any more.'

'No, it's not at all. How could I ever forget you? This lake, the trees, the boats, all remind me of our times together, now and as children. No-one can replace you, so it's you or no-one. Now, there's an ultimatum. I want to be engaged to you and we'll sort out all the problems as we go along. I'll send your step-mother into exile. I'll put her on a ship to a foreign country. I can ask the King to do anything. Besides which, I need to see if this ring fits you.' James pulled a small package out of his pocket, opened it up and asked for Gabriella's hand.

'James,' said Gabriella with her hand behind her back, 'I want to say yes. Are you sure we will sort the problems out first before you make arrangements for us to be married, even if it takes a long time?'

'Yes. I can deal with the problems if I have hope, but not if I'm in despair. Now, give me your hand.'

Gabriella dried her tears on her handkerchief, curtseyed in mock politeness and held out her hand.

'I should think so.' James put the small ring on her finger and it fitted perfectly. He pulled her to him and hugged her tightly. Gabriella put her arms about him and, perforce, laid her head on his shoulder. 'Thank goodness for that,' said James.

From somewhere in the bushes a cheer was heard but was quickly suppressed. James looked exasperated but laughed anyway, and Gabriella hid her smiles in James's coat.

A little later Gabriella entered the back gate of her home and ran in to see if Nanny was on her own in the kitchen. She was, but Nanny looked at her anxiously. 'Nanny, look,' whispered Gabriella and she held out her hand. 'It's secret at the moment so I will have to wear this ring on a chain round my neck but it's good news, I think.'

Nanny burst into tears. 'Thank goodness, child, you had the sense to say yes. I was worried you would not. I'm going to miss you badly but your life will be much better and I won't have to worry about you.'

'Did you know James was going to ask me then?'

'I guessed. So when are you to leave me?'

'Nothing is settled yet, Nanny, and we cannot get married until we have sorted out some problems.' Gabriella did not outline all of them. She did not say anything about Nanny and Mr. Georges coming to the Palace with her either, in case it proved impossible to rectify the problems. Gabriella mentioned wanting a dowry. ‘But there is nothing I can do about that.’

‘I’m not so sure about that, Gabriella. Come with me and see.’

Chapter Twenty

Gabriella had to forget her own plans for two weeks while she prepared for Matilda's wedding. It was not in Gabriella's nature to wish her step-sister ill, so she decided to make this occasion a happy one, if she could.

'How would you like the flowers to be arranged, Matilda?' asked Gabriella one morning while brushing Matilda's hair.

Matilda wanted exotic flowers which were not in season, so rather than say outright that she could not have them, Gabriella suggested some alternatives which would look prettier. When it came to the matter of wedding clothes, it took all Gabriella's tact to get Matilda to accept that she could look pretty without miles of lace veils or several necklaces of gold.

'Where will you live after you are married?' Gabriella asked, in an attempt to show an interest.

'Roland has a mansion somewhere near Derville. He says it has been in the family for centuries and has extensive grounds. The gardens are laid out as woodland at present.'

Gabriella hoped that ancient did not mean falling down, or that woodland did not mean left to go wild. She was of the opinion that a bride should know the home she would be living in after her wedding so that there were no shocks or disappointments.

'I expect you will be able to buy yourself some new clothes after your wedding. I'm packing those which you will not need in the next two weeks but you will need to buy yourself some winter things before the end of the summer. Most of what you have now is too small.'

'Roland is a relative of the King so he will have plenty of money. I will have lots of new gowns and everything I need. I am planning to redecorate the mansion. I expect to be entertaining grand people, Gabriella. I know you will be jealous, but I can't help that.'

Gabriella said simply that she hoped Matilda would be happy.

'And why shouldn't I be?'

Gabriella did not reply. In the following days, using some of her dwindling savings, Gabriella bought Matilda a new petticoat and some pretty nightclothes trimmed with lace. Mrs. Valencie had run out of money after buying a wedding gown and veil. Matilda did not say thank you, but Gabriella had not expected her to do so.

Nanny was also having difficulties. 'There is so little money to make a proper wedding breakfast, Gabriella. What am I to do?'

'The guest list is small, Nanny, so I expect we will manage. There are vegetables in the garden to make soup. Add plenty of water,' Gabriella said with a grin. 'We have a supply of flour in the cupboard. If I pick some wild raspberries, can you make some tartlets?'

'Yes, that's a good idea. But what about a wedding cake? I should have made the cake weeks ago. I could still make one now if I had the ingredients. There's a small amount of brandy left in the cellar which will add a bit of flavour.'

'If you give me a list I'll go to James's uncle's place and see if he has some dried fruit he can let me have for a reasonable price. It will all work out well, Nanny, somehow.'

* * *

Meanwhile James had time to think about Gabriella's problems. He was anxious to find solutions quickly before Gabriella could think there was no hope.

It was not easy to think of what he could do but, in the belief that if he started to look for solutions they would appear out of the blue, James decided to visit Mr. Browning, the solicitor. Once James was ensconced in the solicitor's chair he approached the subject carefully.

'I can rely upon your discretion, of course,' started James.

'Of course,' said Mr. Browning, hoping James had not got a young woman into trouble. Thus he was relieved when he discovered that James was interested in discovering a way to prevent Mrs. Valencie from spreading rumours.

'First of all, may I offer my congratulations, my dear Sir,' began Mr. Browning. 'I am delighted to hear of Miss Valencie's engagement. It is the very thing for her. And you, of course.'

'Yes, thank you, but you must know that Gabriella is very concerned about her father's reputation and will not allow me to make arrangements for our marriage until I have some proof of her father's good reputation or, failing that, something to prevent rumours. I do not know where to start and hoped you would have some idea. My biggest worry is that it may be true that her father was involved in gaming. I knew Mr. Valencie very well, of course, and I cannot believe he would be capable of doing such a thing, but I also know that if he had wanted to hide something he could have done it.'

'I may be able to help you, Sir, but you will understand that Mrs. Valencie is a client of mine and, unfortunately, I cannot discuss her affairs with you. I do, however, want to help, given that Miss Gabriella is also a client. I believe I can assure you that Mr. Valencie was not what Mrs. Valencie is now suggesting. However, I can understand that you will want proof. Can you give me a week or two to think about the situation? I believe there is a solution, but as you can imagine I want to make sure it is legal and air-tight, so to speak.'

'Well, that's a relief at least. Is there anything I can do in the meantime?' asked James. 'I am anxious to do whatever can be done as quickly as possible.'

'At this point, Sir, can I also rely upon your discretion? If I were to ask you to do something, is it possible to guarantee that it does not get back to the person in question?'

'Of course you can. I don't want to create any further problems.'

'In that case, I need to find out where Mrs. Valencie goes in the evenings. I know she visits friends, but which ones and why, I do not know. Some of her outings will undoubtedly be innocent but I have reason to believe that on the odd occasion she may be doing something, let us say, not quite ethical. I should not really be telling you this and I may be wrong about the situation but, as a solicitor, I cannot condone wrongdoing, even in my own clients. I have not been able to send my clerk to follow her because she knows him. Can you help with this?'

'It would be hard for me to follow her because I myself am followed everywhere by a guardsman. There's one down the road at the moment waiting for me, although he does not know I know that. Can you imagine the confusion, with so many people following each other around the town?'

The solicitor looked amused. 'I can indeed.'

'But there is a young officer who is very reliable and I can trust him to report directly to me and to keep quiet about the matter. I would arrange it with the Captain.'

'I am loath to let too many people know about this matter, but if you believe you can get this young officer to do the job without giving anyone too much information, or using my name, I'd be grateful.'

'I'll tell the Captain that I need the officer for some work of my own. The Captain knows that I am involved in some other investigations at present so he will think it is for that. The officer, Smithick, is totally reliable.'

James left the solicitor. Neither he nor the solicitor was totally satisfied with the interview. The solicitor thought so much could go wrong with the plan and James was not happy about the amount of time it was going to take to sort things out. But no other solution had presented itself.

It was also time for James to be making plans to foil Roland's plot at the ball.

Chapter Twenty One

The day of Matilda's wedding came and Gabriella was up early to make the final preparations. She went into the garden for a few precious moments, pleased it was a fine day. The sun was just above the horizon turning the sky all colours. Birds sang happily. Gabriella pondered why life could not always be this peaceful. She sipped the cup of tea she had taken with her and wondered if this day would bring any changes to her own life. All too soon she heard Nanny in the kitchen.

After the frenzy of putting the final touches to the food, taking breakfast trays and hot water upstairs, helping Matilda dress, finding things which were mislaid, keeping all three ladies calm, Gabriella saw them into the carriage Roland had sent to take them to the chapel. Gabriella put on her own simple dress and walked arm-in-arm with Nanny to the little chapel where Roland's wedding party was already assembled. Roland, dressed in a new coat, waited with a few other young men at the front while Matilda fussed over her flowers and train. Gabriella helped her straighten her dress, returned a stray rose to its proper place and sent Matilda down the aisle on the arm of Mr. Georges who had been pressed into giving her away. Gabriella and Nanny sat at the back.

The ceremony began and the young minister read the service slowly. He got to the part where he was to direct his words to to Matilda, 'Please repeat after me: I call upon these persons her present to witness that I . . .,' when Matilda coughed. The minster stopped speaking in alarm but Matilda waved him on. She repeated the words somewhat incoherently, spluttering as she did so, but everyone supposed she was nervous. Eventually though, both Roland and Matilda said 'I do', and the bridal party proceeded into a side room with two of Roland's companions who were to act as witnesses while the register was being signed.

Gabriella prepared to leave with Nanny to get ready for their guests. But before she left her seat, she heard loud voices coming from the side room.

Nanny gave Gabriella a worried look. 'What's happening?' she whispered.

'I don't know, but we'd better wait a minute or two.'

The door to the side room flew open and the minister came out looking flustered. He walked to the back of the chapel and Gabriella was surprised to see him heading for her. 'Can you come with me, Miss Gabriella?' he whispered. 'I won't keep you a moment.'

Gabriella followed him nervously. She thought back to see if she had forgotten to do something for Matilda but could think of nothing. The minister ushered her into the room and closed the door.

'Mr. Roland, Sir, this is Miss Gabriella,' said the minister.

'That's not Miss Gabriella Valencie,' said Roland angrily. 'That's the maid. She was sitting at the back of the chapel with the housekeeper. You've just put the wrong name on the register, which is what I have been saying all along.'

'I copied the names onto the register from the birth certificates I was given. Perhaps Miss Gabriella can explain the misunderstanding.' The minister looked to Gabriella, hoping for an answer.

'What seems to be the problem, Sir?' Gabriella, who was totally confused, turned to Roland.

'The minister has put the wrong name on the register,'

said Roland impatiently. 'This lady's name is Gabriella Valencie but I note here that she is named Matilda.'

'No, that is correct, Sir,' said Gabriella. 'Your bride is named Matilda,'

'She told me her name was Gabriella. Now please, minister, correct the name on these papers.'

'I'm very sorry, sir, but you seem to be under a misapprehension,' said Gabriella quietly. 'I am Gabriella Valencie.'

'No, that is not right,' insisted Roland. 'You are the maid. How many times did I visit this lady's home to find you clearing out the fire or dusting or whatever it is that maids do. You most certainly are not Miss Gabriella. Miss Gabriella Valencie, the daughter of Mr. Valencie who is a relative of the King, would not be doing the work of a maid. Your name could easily be *Cinder*-ella but certainly not Gabriella.'

The minister looked up in surprise. 'Is this true, Miss Gabriella? Have you been involved in the upkeep of the house?'

'It is true I have been helping, but how this gentleman could become so mistaken I cannot understand. This gentleman saw me once at the Palace when I had been invited to one of the Queen's small parties, so surely he knows who I am.'

'I have never met this young lady at the Palace,' said Roland, although he began to have some doubts.

'I can assure you, Sir,' said the Minister, 'that this is Miss Gabriella. The young lady you have married is Miss Matilda.'

'But when I visited this lady's house I requested the maid to fetch the eldest Miss Valencie. I have been reliably informed that there is only one Miss Valencie and her name is Gabriella. Other daughters might not have been registered yet but the eldest is definitely named Gabriella. Maybe your middle name is Gabriella,' suggested Roland to Matilda.

'Matilda is the eldest, Sir,' said Gabriella. 'She is older than

I by a few months. However she is not the daughter of my father but the daughter of the lady my father married after my mother died. Matilda is my step-sister.'

'What?' gasped Roland. 'I came here in good faith, thinking I was marrying Miss Gabriella Valencie only to find now that this is not the case. I have been badly deceived and this marriage is not valid.' Roland sat down and put his head in his hands. He had just remembered that he had asked Matilda if he might call her Gabriella. She had not objected, but not once had anyone told him her name was Gabriella. He had simply assumed it was. Everything was going wrong.

'But it doesn't matter what my name is,' cried Matilda. 'It's me you want to marry. What does it matter what my name is? I have now changed it to your name anyway. You can call me Gabriella if you want.'

Roland said nothing but continued to hold his head.

'Why is it so important that my sister's name should be Gabriella?' asked Gabriella.

Roland said nothing

'Well,' said Gabriella. 'There may have been a small mix-up. But my step-sister is correct, Sir. Matilda is the one you asked to marry and she is the very one here today and, as far as I can see, is now your wife.'

'No,' mumbled Roland.

'The vows have been said and the register signed, Sir,' said the minister. 'Miss Matilda is most definitely your wife. I must say that I believe your conduct in this matter is not good. You are upsetting the young lady and on her wedding day too. Now, Sir, I ask you to put on a better face and proceed with your guests who are waiting patiently outside. You will find that this young lady will make you an excellent wife, I am sure.'

Matilda was in tears but Gabriella could see that she was angry more than upset. Gabriella took a handkerchief out of her purse and gave it to Matilda. 'Now listen, both of you. What the minister has said is correct. Both of you will now smile and enjoy the little reception we have arranged. Otherwise you are going to be the talk of the town. We can sort out any problems afterwards. So let me go first. I will ask everyone to come to our house and will start to arrange some refreshments. You will take a little time to compose yourselves and follow as quickly as you can. I will make things as smooth as I can.'

With that Gabriella left them, shutting the door after her. She could see that Mrs. Valencie was coming over to her to ask what the problem was, so Gabriella quickly announced in a loud voice that the bride and groom would be delighted if everyone would proceed to Mrs. Valencie's home and they would follow shortly. She said Mr. Georges would give anyone directions should they not know the way. Gabriella found Nanny and escaped out of the chapel as fast as she could.

'What happened, Gabriella?' asked Nanny.

'I'll tell you later, Nanny. I just do not know how this situation arose or why, but I'm going to have to find out. My main concern now is to keep the guests so busy that they don't question what is going on. We will set out the food as soon as we can.'

'A glass or two of wine will help the guests, Gabriella.'

'It might help us too' said Gabriella grimly. Nanny laughed.

* * *

Gabriella greeted each guest with a bright smile, took their coats and directed them to the drawing room where Mr. Georges was handing out glasses of wine. Mrs. Rodriguez waited until the last guest had arrived, then quietly asked Gabriella what she could do to help.

'Thank you very much, Mrs. Rodriguez. I know you will be wondering what is going on but I cannot say too much at present.'

'My only aim, Gabriella, is to help. I do not have to know your business, dear girl.'

'I know, and I am so sorry to be discourteous. I note that it is very quiet in the drawing room. Would you be so kind as to start a conversation with someone? It might help.'

'Of course,' said Mrs. Rodriguez. 'I know exactly what to do. Will we be eating soon? How long do I have to keep everyone occupied?'

'Not long. Nanny has the dining room ready and as soon as I am finished here I will bring the food to the table. Fortunately we could not seat everyone at the table so people must help themselves to some food and sit wherever they can. This way we do not have to wait for the newly-weds to arrive. It would be better if they were here, but I can make some excuse.'

Mrs. Rodriguez went into the drawing room, asked the nearest lady where she was from and then introduced her to the next lady, gradually including more people into the conversation until everyone had been introduced to each other. Polite enquires were made as the quests asked after each others' well-being, the travel arrangements each had made and so on until Mr. Georges announced that lunch had been served. This gave everyone something to do and the atmosphere improved.

Gabriella took empty plates to the kitchen, resupplied the table and was generally rushed off her feet. In the middle of all this, Matilda and Roland entered the house accompanied by the minister. Roland looked stormy, Matilda's eyes were red and the minister had an air of determination.

'Well now,' said the minister heartily. 'Here we are, at last. At least, we have not kept everyone waiting.'

'No, I thought it best to proceed,' said Gabriella. 'Please step into the library where we can leave the flowers.' She ushered them into the small room before imploring Matilda and Roland to do their best to appear happy. 'Whatever has gone wrong can be dealt with later. I have done my best to keep your guests entertained but you need to greet them yourselves. Please make them believe everything is as it should be. I need to help Matilda wash her face for a moment. Perhaps, Sirs, you will be good enough to proceed to the dining room.'

Gabriella pushed Matilda up the stairs where a bowl of warm water was waiting. Matilda was inclined to pour out all her troubles but Gabriella did to have time to listen.

'Please, Matilda, not now. I have a house full of people to cope with. You must do your part. You have what you wanted. If you put on a sour face you might drive Roland away completely.'

Matilda saw it made sense, so it was not long before Gabriella was able to present her to the guests. Matilda's bad mood turned into a gaiety which, although a little forced, was better than tears. Roland smiled more through his teeth than anything but Gabriella had to be satisfied with that.

It was probably one of the quickest wedding breakfasts ever. As soon as everyone had eaten something and congratulated the happy couple, guests made their excuses and left, until the only one left was the minister. Gabriella prepared herself for the worst.

The storm broke as Roland said icily that he would leave them now and they would hear from his lawyer as soon as he could arrange for the marriage to be annulled. Matilda gasped.

'I do not think it will be as easy as that,' said the minister.

'No, certainly not,' said Mrs. Valencie, who had by this time been appraised of the situation. 'You will hear from our lawyer too. We will claim breach of promise, neglect, desertion, and anything else I can think of. My dear daughter will be asking for a lot of money to compensate her for the suffering you have put her through.'

Roland was about to argue and Matilda too added her

protests, but Gabriella had had enough. Florence was giggling in the corner until Gabriella sent her an angry look.

'We are not accomplishing anything by arguing now. What Matilda needs to know is where she is going to be staying tonight. I believe, Sir, you had rooms booked in a small hostelry on your way to Derville, and I suggest this plan continues. It will look very odd to the neighbours if you, Sir, leave without her. Our butler has loaded all her belongings into your carriage which is now waiting for you both.'

'I'm not taking her with me. She deceived me completely.'

'I did not!' Matilda almost shouted but Gabriella shushed her quickly.

'In this instance, Sir, I believe my step-sister is correct. Take your bride with you, which is the proper thing to do. You will suit each other well and once you have both calmed down you will see that the life you have chosen is not so bad after all.'

The minister agreed, and with that the couple were put into their cloaks hastily. Matilda was helped into the carriage and Roland, without a glance at Matilda, took the reins.

Gabriella thanked the minister for his help and told him she would speak to him as soon as she had time in the next day or two. He shook her hand, gave her a look of sympathy, and walked away shaking his head.

Gabriella avoided the drawing room where she knew Mrs. Valencie was waiting for her, and went to the kitchen. She emptied a kettle of water into the sink and started to wash the empty plates and glasses. Nanny put her arm around her and gave her a hug but neither said anything.

Chapter Twenty Two

The following day started badly. Mrs. Valencie complained loudly to Gabriella, saying she would visit the solicitor as soon as she was dressed. Gabriella was to help her get ready before she did anything else.

While Mrs. Valencie drank a cup of hot chocolate, Florence got under Gabriella's feet, asking a lot of questions in a hoarse whisper. Gabriella ignored her. However, before long Mrs. Valencie walked out of the house with Florence, who was to visit the library while Mrs. Valencie spoke to the solicitor.

Gabriella wrote a quick note and sent Susie to the Palace to deliver it. Within half an hour Nanny heard a quiet knock at the back door.

'Do come in, Sir,' said Nanny to James. 'It's not fitting that you should come to the back door but Gabriella will be grateful if the neighbours do not know you are visiting. Perhaps you will come up to the drawing room.'

'No, I'll stay here, Nanny, thank you. If I need to leave quickly it will be easier from here.'

'Oh dear,' said Nanny, fussing with a clean cushion for the Prince. 'The kitchen is really not the place for you, I am so sorry.'

'Nanny, I have sat in this kitchen numerous times and very good times they were too. Being Prince is just a job of work, exactly like yours. I am very comfortable, thank you. Is Gabriella here? She needed to speak to me.'

'Yes, of course. I was forgetting. I'll fetch her now and leave you to talk.'

As Gabriella entered the kitchen James rose, caught her hands and kissed them. He looked worried. 'What is the problem, dear one? Please tell me.'

'It may be nothing, but it is lovely to see you, so that is a blessing. The problem is this.' Gabriella told James about Roland and the mistake over Matilda's name. 'I am mystified as to why he would want to marry me, or rather, someone with the name Gabriella Valencie? Can you tell me?'

'I have no idea at all.' James thought for a moment. 'But I can ask Mr. Secretary and, if he does not know, I can ask the King. One or the other will know. It's most odd.'

'Do you think he believes I have inherited a fortune after my father died?'

'He may have done, but did he ask Matilda or Mrs. Valencie about money? It would be usual for an enquiry to be made about financial matters. Or maybe he spoke to the solicitor.'

'If he spoke to the solicitor he would know that neither I nor Matilda has anything. I asked the solicitor myself. My step-mother has control of the money, and there appears to be precious little of it.'

'So it must be something else. Give me a few hours and I will see what I can find out. But while I am here tell me how you are.'

'Strained, but I'm beginning to see the funny side of all this.'

'I'm glad to see you smiling at last.'

Just before he left James remembered he was to ask Gabriella to visit the Queen. 'She was so happy about our engagement that she wanted to hold an engagement party. I told her it would not be good just yet but she wants to speak with you. When do you think you can come? Would now be a good time? I can escort you to the Palace.'

So Gabriella put on a pretty dress, threw an old cloak over it, grabbed a basket and walked out with James.

The Queen was making pastry but quickly washed her hands and hugged Gabriella. 'My dear girl, I am so delighted about your news. Now I know you cannot stay long. Just two things; I have a little present for you.' The Queen gave Gabriella a parcel. 'And I want you to visit the shoe-maker in the village. He will explain why. He is expecting you.'

Gabriella took the parcel and put it in her basket. 'I cannot thank you enough, Ma'am. I am worried . . .'

The Queen did not allow her to say anything else. 'I know, dear, but things will work out well. We would like to arrange a more formal meeting for you with myself and the King, when you and James let us do it.' She smiled kindly.

Gabriella walked to the shoe-maker to find he wanted to measure her feet. 'What is this for, if I may ask?'

'The Queen wants you to have a pretty pair of dancing shoes. It is a little gift to you. I will need you to visit me next week, if you will,' said the shoe-maker.

Gabriella now worried that if her engagement had to be cancelled she would be in debt to the Queen. She decided to ask James to mention this to the Queen. 'I wonder if I might ask you to be very discreet about these shoes.'

'I have been sworn to secrecy,' said the shoe-maker laughing. 'So here is an old pair of shoes which need throwing away. It will look as if you came here for shoe repairs.'

Gabriella reflected that there were a lot of things being kept secret. Sooner or later it would all be out in the open.

* * *

James told Mr. Secretary the story of Roland's wedding.

Mr. Secretary raised his eyes in surprise. 'I need to think about this, if you can give me a moment.'

So James sat quietly.

The secretary took a book from a shelf. 'I just want to check something,' he said.

James waited patiently while the secretary turned pages.

Eventually, the secretary closed the book. 'I believe this is more serious than appears on the surface. With your permission, James, I will inform the King. It may be an urgent matter, but we will see.'

'Is Gabriella in danger?' asked James getting anxious.

'I do not believe so. You stated that Roland is definitely married and will not be able to get a divorce quickly. And he has travelled back home to Grelland, so he is out of the way at present, which means Miss Gabriella is safe. But we need to make sure that remains the case.'

'But why is Gabriella likely to be in danger?'

'Let me ask the King if he is available to talk to us. If you will wait for a few minutes I will inform the King of the situation.' Mr. Secretary rose from his chair.

James was left to pace up and down the secretary's office for half an hour until Jenny came to ask him to attend the King in the Library.

'Come in, James, and thank you, Jenny.' The King was sitting at his writing desk. Mr. Secretary sat on a chair across the room. 'Well now, we do not want you to worry too much about this situation, but it needs to be watched carefully. Given the attacks on your person, James, we must conclude that Roland has designs on the throne of Essenia.'

'Yes, thank you, Sir,' said James, 'but I am at a loss to understand why that is the case, and why there is some danger for Gabriella.'

'I can answer one of those questions. Obviously you have not studied your family's genealogical records. If Gabriella had been a son to Mr. Valencie instead of a daughter, she, or rather he, would have been the heir to the throne, not you. Gabriella is closer to the throne than you. You are related to her distantly, although by so many cousins removed that it would not affect your marriage. But it appears that Roland, by marrying Miss Gabriella, wanted to strengthen his ties to the throne. As to why, I have no idea. We need to find out as quickly as possible.'

Mr. Secretary added that if they could understand why Roland wanted to be King of Essenia, it would help to thwart any plans to that end.

'So is Gabriella in any danger?' James asked.

'She is safe while Roland is out of the country, but if he came back Gabriella could be vulnerable while she is living at home. She ventures out on her own to go to the market and is often to be seen in her garden, which has no security whatsoever.'

'Yes, I know. All you have to do is walk in the back gate.'

'However, we do not consider there to be any serious danger because we cannot see what Roland can do to her that would be to his advantage, now that he is safely married. So, purely as a precautionary measure, we would like her to make plans to come to live with us. She will be coming to live with us soon anyway, which we are delighted about. You know the Queen will make her very comfortable.'

'I know and it is very much appreciated, but Gabriella would not allow it, Sir,' said James. He then related the problem Gabriella had with her step-mother and her father's reputation.

The King was astounded. 'Do you really mean to say this woman would spread such false rumours?'

'It seems likely, Sir. Gabriella does not believe it is enough to know her father was innocent of the claims his widow is making. She would prefer to have proof of the matter. I am working towards finding the proof with the help of the solicitor in the town. But it's not only that. Gabriella will not desert her housekeeper and the butler.'

'For the present then, if Roland returns to Essenia we will place a guard on Gabriella. You may like to warn her of the event so that she is not worried about being followed. It is unfortunate that we cannot cancel Roland's invitation to the ball, but maybe we can turn that to our advantage. Now, tell me what plans are being made for your safety at the ball.'

Chapter Twenty Three

James gave the young officer of the guard, Sam Smithick, a free hand to do whatever was necessary to discover any information concerning Mrs. Valencie. Sam understood the matter was urgent.

He decided to follow Mrs. Valencie all day, not just in the evenings, in case her behaviour was suspect at other times. But Sam found that following someone was not as easy as he had thought it would be. He had to stay out of Mrs. Valencie's sight which meant that frequently he lost her. The first time he lost her he ran to the end of a street only to find her immediately around the corner looking into a shop window. He then had to stroll nonchalantly past her, which meant he lost her again. Loitering about on the first day of his detective work made other people suspicious, such as the market stall holder who believed Sam was about to steal something. The vendor accosted him and told him to clear off. It drew attention to Sam which was the opposite of what he wanted.

From then on Sam wore his uniform. He strode importantly around the market place and up and down surrounding streets. The market stall holder told Sam he was glad to see him as he was sure there were thieves about.

Mrs. Valencie did nothing unusual the first day. She visited the market for small items and then proceeded to the library. She returned home and stayed at home for the rest of the day.

The following day, Sam followed Mrs. Valencie to a home on the edge of town where she was invited in. Sam marched past the house to the corner of the road, stopped and took out a notebook and importantly wrote a note in it. But he could not stay on that corner for long so had to walk away. He lost Mrs. Valencie after that but guessed she would stay at home for the afternoon. In the evening, Sam patrolled the area near Mrs. Valencie's home but she did not venture out. Just after midnight, Sam decided it would be safe for him to go home for the night.

For the next day, Sam chanced wearing old clothes. He borrowed a brush and shovel from a road sweeper and cleaned the road outside the house Mrs. Valencie had visited yesterday. Sam brushed the road and path meticulously, albeit very slowly. The only problem he encountered was from a man who, as he passed by, said he hoped the lad would not overtax himself.

Mrs. Valencie passed Sam on her way to the house, stayed there for an hour and left only when the doctor arrived. Over the next few days Sam was able to discover that Mrs. Valencie often visited this house in the mornings.

It was not until the Wednesday of the second week that Mrs. Valencie left her home in the evening. She was invited into another house, this time in the centre of the town. Sam, once again in his uniform, was able to patrol the area well because twilight and then darkness made his activities less noticeable. He watched others, more men than women, enter the house. Mrs. Valencie did not leave until the early hours of the next morning. She was a little unsteady on her feet.

Sam believed he had something to report but wanted to find out more about the house on the edge of town. It took him three more days to become acquainted with the kitchen maid.

* * *

Roland had driven Matilda away from Mrs. Valencie's house in a temper. At times Matilda thought the carriage would be overturned and shouted at Roland to slow down. It made things worse and he urged the horses on. However, as the road took twists and turns Roland realised his own life was at stake so took the corners more carefully. At the posting inn, Roland ignored Matilda completely. That evening she ordered herself a meal to be served in her room. Roland stayed in the saloon until the early hours of the next morning.

Matilda realised that shouting at Roland did no good. It even made things worse. So for the present she decided to concentrate on surviving the journey to Grelland where she could decide on her next move. Even at the places Roland stopped to allow the horses a rest, Roland and Matilda hardly spoke a word to each other.

They arrived at Roland's home in darkness. Matilda only had time to find a few of her belongings and take herself to bed. The old housekeeper had prepared a room for her where a small fire sputtered feebly in the grate.

For the next few days Roland was missing. Matilda wandered through the house, noticing the faded drapes, the broken furniture, threadbare carpets and broken stairs. The longer Roland stayed away the angrier Matilda got. To make matters worse the housekeeper's cooking was so bad, Matilda couldn't eat much. Hunger made her temper flare. She longed for Gabriella's cooking. One morning she flounced out of the house and paced around the garden. The hedges needed trimming, a stone wall had tumbled down and saplings were taking root in what had once been a lawn. She argued with the young lad who looked after the one horse left in the stables, telling him he should not be so lazy and asked why he was not keeping the garden tidy. The lad said he didn't get paid to do the gardening.

Irately, Matilda went into the house and found Roland's

library. She searched everywhere, in drawers, on the desktop and among the shelves. She found nothing to help her. Then she thought of Roland's dressing room.

She was not surprised to find many expensive coats hanging there, and as she whisked through them, she felt into each of the pockets, but they were all empty. It was when she poked through Roland's collection of shoes that she noticed a large tin hidden in a corner. She picked it up and took it to her room.

The tin opened easily and she emptied the contents onto the bed. A few letters came out and on top of them fell several sovereigns. Matilda quickly pocketed the sovereigns and flicked through the letters most of which were from Roland's man of business. These were of no interest to Matilda except that they bore the business man's address in St. Mary's Road, Derville. She put one of the letters in her pocket with the money and took the tin back to the dressing room.

Matilda went down to the kitchen to find the housekeeper and asked her to spare a few minutes. The housekeeper slowly wiped her hands and stood before Matilda anxiously.

'I want to know why we do not have more staff,' said Matilda.

'Yes, madam, of course. You see, most of the time the master is not here so we do not need very much help.'

'But the garden needs attending to and so does the house.'

'The master did employ some people for a short time but they left, I'm afraid.'

'And why was that?'

'Well, madam, I wouldn't like to talk out of turn.'

'Tell me, if you please.'

'Yes, you see, they did not get any money. After a short time they knew they would not be paid and so had to go.'

'Oh, I see. Do you get paid?'

'No, madam, but I am given a little for housekeeping money and I manage, you know. I had nowhere else to go.

I'm old, so no-one would want to hire me. I expect you have noticed that the food is not the best. I have to economise as best I can.

'Yes, I suppose you have. Well, I propose to go out and get some staff this very day.'

'Begging your pardon, madam, but they might not come. This place has a bit of a reputation, sorry. No-one will come if they think they won't be paid.'

'No, of course not. Well, I'll have to pay a little in advance I suppose. Is there an agency in the city? And I need directions to St. Mary's Road.'

The housekeeper gave her the necessary directions and found her mistress a coat and walking shoes. 'Perhaps I'd better come with you, madam. I need some things from the market so I could keep you company and help you on your way.'

In a short time Matilda and the housekeeper set off.

Chapter Twenty Four

Before Matilda's wedding, Nanny had taken Gabriella into the small back room Nanny shared with Mr. Georges. She opened a drawer and felt about at the back of it and brought out a little wooden box.

'Look at these, Gabriella.' Nanny took out a delicate necklace, some earrings and a bracelet. 'They belong to you. I am not sure what the stones are but I expect they are valuable.'

'Where did these come from, Nanny?'

'They were your mother's. Shortly before he died, your father asked me to keep these for you. He was upset about something and asked me to put them in a safe place. He gave me no instructions as to what I was to do with them so I have kept them, thinking that what I should do would become clear in time. And now I believe it is time you had them.'

'Nanny, I do not know what to say.' Gabriella picked up the bracelet and held it against her wrist. 'They are beautiful, but would I ever be able to wear them without my step-mother taking them from me?'

'You will certainly wear them on your wedding day, my dear. What could your step-mother do after that?'

'My father's will is such that everything has been left to her. She would no doubt claim the jewellery as belonging to her. It would cause such an upset for the King and Queen that I could not risk it happening. And my wedding is by no means certain, Nanny. I still have one or two things to make sure of before I can make any such arrangements.'

'What sort of things, Gabriella?'

'Don't worry about anything, Nanny. I will tell you about it if I ever solve the problems.' Gabriella picked up the necklace. 'Something has just occurred to me. Do you think my step-mother was looking for these that day she sent me out?'

'Undoubtedly. I expect she knew they existed, but didn't know where to find them. It wouldn't have occurred to her that the Master would give the jewels into my care. If she had attempted to search my room I would certainly have made a fuss. If, as we think, she is in debt of some sort, and she had found these, she would have sold them or given them to pay the debts.'

'That seems most likely. Thank you so much, Nanny, for taking care of them but you took a huge risk in keeping them. If my step-mother had found them in your possession she would have accused you of stealing. I must think about what to do with them now. I cannot take them to the solicitor because he might give them to my step-mother, if he believed she was entitled to them.'

'They have been safe enough in my drawer.'

'Yes, thank you. You have taken very good care of them but I cannot risk them being found with you now. My step-mother has searched my room so I can hide them there safely for a few days until I work out where to keep them.' Gabriella gave Nanny a quick hug and tucked the box into her apron pocket. Gabriella did not tell Nanny that if she and Mr. Georges were given notice to leave, Gabriella planned to use the jewels to pay for their retirement.

While Gabriella had Matilda's wedding to think about she could not put her mind to the problem of where to keep the jewels, but afterwards she knew it was time to put them somewhere safer than in her room.

The Queen had told Gabriella that she was now one of

the family and must visit whenever she wanted. So when Gabriella was sure Mrs. Valencie was resting in her room and Florence had gone to visit a friend, she set off for the Palace. She took the small wooden box with her.

James was working in the kitchen that week and as Gabriella entered the Palace's back gate she found him washing carrots in the kitchen garden. This was the first time Gabriella had come to the Palace without a specific invitation so James was surprised but very pleased to see her.

He bounded over to meet her and kissed her cheek with his hands waving about in the air. 'I need to wash my hands, Gabriella. Do please come into the kitchen and I will take you up to the drawing room in a minute.'

'I cannot stay long, James, so we can stay in the garden if you don't mind.'

'If you would like to sit on a garden chair then, I will just tell Jenny to bring some tea. You must have something.'

James hurried to the kitchen and soon came out with a tray. 'The Queen had some soup ready for dinner and wants you to try it. She'll give us some time to ourselves.' He pulled a metal table close, set the tray on it and urged her to eat. 'Now, Gabriella, I expect something is urgent, so please tell me if I can help.'

Gabriella took a sip of her soup. 'This is lovely, thank you. I didn't have time for lunch today. What I really came about is this.' She handed James the wooden box and he opened it.

'Oh,' he said, drawing in his breath quickly. 'What are you doing, Gabriella, walking about with a fortune in your basket?'

'With me dressed like this, no-one would think I had anything valuable on me.'

'I'm not so sure. You look wonderful in anything, Gabriella. You certainly don't look like one of the servants. But do tell me where these came from.'

'It's a long story.' Gabriella told James how the jewellery

had come into her possession. 'I cannot keep them at home any longer but I do not know where to put them. I do not believe they are very valuable but I could sell them in an emergency.'

'You can't sell these, Gabriella. Your mother wanted you to have them, obviously. But I believe them to be diamonds. The stones might seem small to you, but as diamonds go they are quite large. The settings are probably gold.' James looked at the bracelet carefully. 'Yes, look, there is a mark here.'

'That just makes it more important that I keep them somewhere safe. Please can you keep them here?' Gabriella did not have time to argue with James, that she would sell the items if Nanny needed the money.

'I expect we could find somewhere for them. At least it's solved the problem of your dowry, not that you needed one. You can give them to the crown and then we can give them back to you to wear on state occasions.'

'But I am still no further forward with the other difficulties.'

'As it happens we are a little further forward. I was hoping to see you soon because we have a little news from the solicitor.'

'Is there really? James, please do tell me.'

'It might not be much, so don't be disappointed. Anyway, you will not be very surprised to learn that your step-mother goes to card games. She visits a place where we know the stakes are high.'

Gabriella stopped eating. 'Are you sure?'

'We know she goes to the place but, of course, we have no proof as yet that she takes part in the gaming. But there would be no other reason for her to go there. The only thing we find hard to understand is why she is allowed to continue going there. She is obviously in debt and usually would not be welcomed until the debts are paid off. The only thing we can think of is that she has promised to pay the debts when your father's will is finalised. In the meantime, maybe she is hoping to win enough to pay off the debt. It wouldn't be the first time a gambler tried to do that.'

'That's disastrous news. The solicitor said the will's completion could take two years, but it might take less time. Once it comes back we will be worse off than now. I have no idea how much my step-mother owes, but it is sure to be a large amount. She will use the principle and then there will be very little in the way of interest for us to live on.'

'It doesn't matter, Gabriella, because you will be here with me. So will Nanny and Mr. Georges. All we have to do is inform your step-mother that we know she goes to these gaming places and we think it will keep her quiet.'

'Maybe, but I would still be anxious about it. She might say she was forced into it after my father got us into so much trouble.'

'I suppose she could. I can see the problem you have. We do have a little hope though, because the solicitor says he is still making enquires. I wish there was something else I could do.'

'You have done so much already. I'm sure it will lead towards a solution eventually.'

'Actually, there is a bit more news.'

'There is? James, please don't keep me in suspense.' Gabriella put down her spoon.

'It seems your step-mother is hoping to marry again to solve her problems.'

'What? Are you serious? How did you discover that?'

'It's a long story but it seems to be credible enough.'

'I find that very surprising. No-one has been visiting our house, except that horrible man who shouts at her. I don't think she would marry him.'

'No, not him. Your step-mother has been visiting someone who has been ill for some time. The kitchen staff and the butler are most put out about it. They say she is worming her way into the household. She takes sweetmeats in with her and other little things and keeps telling this elderly gentleman that she wishes she could look after him all the time.'

'Is he wealthy?'

'Of course.'

'That makes things a little difficult for me.'

'Why?'

'It makes the future unsure. Suppose my step-mother were to sell our home. I would be left without anywhere to live because it is unlikely I would be able to live in this other gentleman's home. I'd refuse to go anyway. I could sell the jewellery and make a home for Nanny and Mr. Georges with me. But my step-mother would ask where the money came from and then she would claim that money back as her right according to my father's will.'

'Yes, I suppose it would make things precarious. Are you certain you would not come to live with me and let the King deal with any rumours your step-mother might spread?'

'I just could not do that. I want to bring good things with me, not bad.'

James sighed. 'I suppose I can understand that. So let's see what the solicitor discovers.'

'I think it is time I released you from this engagement. I was wrong to let it happen.'

'Oh no, you weren't. That's the worst thing that you could do. Give it time, Gabriella. I couldn't cope if you left me now. You don't want to leave me, do you?"

Gabriella sank back in her chair. 'I can't think of anything worse,' she whispered.

James grinned. 'I thought so.'

Chapter Twenty Five

Matilda left her housekeeper at the market and found Roland's man of business. She was invited into a small, austere office. It felt cold after the warmth of the sun outside.

The accountant congratulated her on her marriage, of which he had been informed by Roland.

'I am here,' she started, 'because my husband has had to leave suddenly on an urgent errand, but he forgot to leave me any money with which to manage the household. I wish to hire more staff in order to run the place as it should be done.'

'Well, Madam, your husband has given me some instructions, naturally, when he informed me of your forthcoming marriage.'

'Good,' said Matilda. 'What were they?'

'You are aware, of course, that your stay at your present address is not to be permanent.'

Matilda was not aware of anything of the sort but she nodded anyway. 'Please go on.'

'So it was not thought expedient to hire staff, which ordinarily would be proper. Your husband hoped you would be comfortable enough with your housekeeper for the few weeks before you move to more suitable accommodation.'

'Oh. As it happens I find it extremely uncomfortable. But if matters are further forward than I thought, then maybe I can bear it.'

'I have been given instructions to sell the house as soon

as your new place is ready. I am sure this news will help you to cope. You may like to prepare for a move instead of putting your energies into the present house. I am sure you will find this a better course than giving yourself a lot of trouble for very little reward.'

'Yes, I expect so. Can you let me have a little money to buy immediate necessities?'

'There is very little on hand at present, I am afraid. But your husband did indicate he would be selling his horse and carriage. Perhaps you may like to give orders to the stable hand who looks after the, um, said articles, to drive them to me for their forthcoming sale. Then, after some debts have been settled, I could give you a little of the residue.'

'Very well. I will do that as soon as I return home. How long will it be before I can have some money?' Matilda had very little need for a carriage. Derville was within walking distance of her home.

'Shall we say two weeks?'

Matilda was disappointed but remembered the sovereigns in her pocket. The accountant saw her out of his premises and she went to find her housekeeper. Once she had located her, Matilda gave her a sovereign to buy some good food. The housekeeper had not seen so much money in a long time and promised to cook some good meals as soon as she had finished her shopping.

* * *

Roland, meanwhile, had taken up residence in an inn as far from Matilda as his finances would allow. He had to think about his disastrous marriage, to make plans to end it and to turn this new situation to his advantage.

Chapter Twenty Six

The solicitor took another trip to Derville and, upon his return, requested an appointment with Prince James. James attended him at his offices. Shortly thereafter, James gave some instructions to the Captain of the Guard. He rose very early the next morning and went to Gabriella's house to find her before Mrs. Valencie should wake up. He found Gabriella lighting a fire to heat water.

'The sooner I get you away from all this the better,' said James. 'Let me help.'

'I've nearly finished, thank you so much, James. Besides which, Florence will be up shortly. She is to visit a friend and it takes her ages to get ready.'

James pulled a face. 'The solicitor needs us to visit him at his offices tomorrow, Gabriella. It's urgent.'

'Is there any news, then?'

'He couldn't tell me much but I think it may work out well. We need to be there by ten in the morning. Can you arrange that?'

'I expect so. Nanny will see to my step-mother for me and make excuses for me. Is there nothing you can tell me?'

'I don't know much. It will be better for the solicitor to explain it all. I might get it wrong. I would like to accompany you to the solicitor but I think you may have to make your own way there, if you don't mind. I'll be waiting there for you.'

The floorboards creaked above their heads and James took his leave after kissing Gabriella's cheek quickly.

* * *

That evening Mrs. Valencie gave Gabriella instructions to bring hot water to her room by half past nine the following morning. 'I have to leave the house quite early,' she said. It complicated Gabriella's planned escape from the house, but Nanny said she would be able to wait on Mrs. Valencie and she would tell Mrs. Valencie that Gabriella had to go to the market for some badly needed provisions.

So Gabriella got up earlier than usual, lit the fire for Nanny and drank a quick cup of tea after the water had boiled. She ran upstairs quietly and put on one of her mother's walking dresses. She covered it with an old, thin shawl. She took the ring from around her neck and put it on her finger. Gabriella hoped it could stay on her finger from now on. She took some hot water up the stairs and left it outside her step-mother's room for Nanny to take in. She grabbed a shopping basket from the kitchen and left the house by the back gate.

Gabriella was invited into the solicitor's office by the clerk, where James was waiting for her. The solicitor shook her hand. James took her arm and led her to a chair at the far side of the solicitor's desk. He sat beside her and smiled as he noted the ring.

'We must wait a few minutes,' said the solicitor. 'But in the meantime I can assure you I believe this is good news. I know you will be impatient to know what it is, but if you would be so kind as to wait a moment or two it will be easier for me to give you the whole story.'

Gabriella had known things to go wrong so many times that she had little faith that this was to be good news. But she settled herself in her chair, resigned herself to whatever was to come and took comfort from James's presence.

After fifteen minutes of talking of the weather and the state of the roads between Essenia and Derville, Gabriella heard movement in the outer office. John, the clerk, ushered in Mrs. Valencie.

Gabriella grabbed James's arm. He reassuringly covered her hand with his own.

Mrs. Valencie stopped short as she saw Gabriella in the room.

'What is my step-daughter doing here, may I ask?' she asked, her voice distinctly chilly.

'Please, Mrs. Valencie, do come in,' said the solicitor. 'All will become clear soon.'

'I do not wish to stay in these circumstances,' said Mrs. Valencie. 'I will speak to Gabriella at home. We can leave now.' Mrs Valencie went to open the door but the clerk stood in her way.

'I am very sorry to have to state, Mrs. Valencie, that you must stay here.' The solicitor nodded to his clerk who helped Mrs. Valencie back into the room and set a chair for her as far as possible from Gabriella.

Gabriella took her hand from under James's and rubbed her eyes with a handkerchief. Mrs Valencie stiffened.

'What is that ring doing on my step-daughter's hand? Are you engaged to someone, Gabriella?'

James shielded Gabriella from Mrs. Valencie's stare. 'I believe all will become clear presently, Mrs. Valencie,' he said.

But Mrs. Valencie stamped her foot. 'I am that girl's guardian and I have not given my permission for her to be engaged to anyone. I demand to be told immediately what is going on. To whom are you engaged, girl?'

Gabriella sat up straighter in her chair but said nothing.

The solicitor intervened. 'That's not important just now, Mrs. Valencie. Please listen to what I have to say first. I can answer your questions later.'

'No, I want to know what is going on,' said Mrs. Valencie in a high voice. 'Obviously it cannot be thought that Gabriella is engaged to Prince James. I forbid any engagement. So Gabriella will return that ring to whoever gave it to her, and come home with me.'

'Mrs. Valencie, please may I ask you to be calm,' said the solicitor. 'I believe, in the wake of what I am to tell you, you will realise that you have no authority whatsoever to make such demands. Now, if you please, I will relate the position to you.'

For the first time Mrs. Valencie's eyes showed a little fear. She clutched the small bag she was carrying and sat back in her chair.

'Thank you,' said the solicitor. 'Now, I have had the necessity to visit Derville on several occasions. What I have discovered is of interest to all present. You, Mrs. Valencie, were married to a Mr. Joshua Sertus.'

Mrs. Valencie nodded. 'My first husband died when one of his merchant ships was shipwrecked. It was such a terrible thing to happen to me and my daughters.'

The solicitor continued. 'I traced his last movements to that ship, of course. I discovered, with the help of my clerk, that Mr. Sertus had done well in his business but suffered disastrous losses towards the end of his career. I found the house in which he spent a little time when away from his family, which was located in the port so as to be near the ship in question.'

Mrs. Valencie acknowledged this.

The solicitor looked up from his books. 'He is still in that house.'

Mrs. Valencie gasped. 'Surely you do not mean his corpse,' she stated.

'No, he is very much alive.'

'That's nonsense,' said Mrs Valencie. 'We had a small funeral service after he was lost in the wreck. One or two sailors survived the disaster but my husband was nowhere to be found.'

'There is a reason for that, Mrs. Valencie. It appears he did not set sail with that ship as you may have believed. Let me tell you the whole story.'

Gabriella had gone back to hanging onto James's arm and the more she heard the more she squeezed. 'Ow,' James whispered into her ear.

Gabriella immediately lessened her hold. 'Sorry,' she whispered back.

'So,' said the solicitor. 'Mr. Sertus found that much of his money was missing but he had trouble finding out where it had gone. He looked into whether thieves had taken it somehow, or if his clerks were dishonest. He found that was not the case. It turned out that his wife had incurred enormous debts and she had cunningly invented large bills. She presented these to her husband's clerks in the accounts office, delivering them by one of her maids. These bills had the names of her creditors on them. The goods being billed were things such as provisions for the ship. The goods did not exist, of course. However, the unsuspecting clerks paid the bills.'

'That is absolutely not true,' exclaimed Mrs. Valencie. 'I did nothing of the sort.'

'Unfortunately, Mrs. Valencie, or should I say Mrs. Sertus, I have an affidavit here signed by your husband declaring the matter to be true. Obviously he did not wish to make such a statement for reasons which I will now explain. I also have written copies of the bills in question, certified by myself. The named creditors existed but their businesses were fictional.'

The clerk still standing at the back of the room heard a slight noise in the outer office. He excused himself for a moment.

'Mr. Sertus,' the solicitor went on, 'in his wisdom, decided that he would pretend to die. In this way he believed he would not be liable for his wife's debts, which were crippling his business. The business was sold ostensibly but no money was made available to the, er, widow. The story was put about that the sale of the business only covered expenses which had accrued. Mrs. Sertus was left to fend for herself. She still had debts and was desperate to find a solution. She then made the acquaintance of Mr. Valencie and you know the rest. A marriage settlement helped with those debts. For a time this apparently newly married lady managed to keep within her allowance but eventually old habits came to the fore and she began to incur more debts.'

'This is absolute nonsense,' Mrs. Valencie almost shouted.

The solicitor held up his hand to indicate to the lady to allow him to proceed. 'Mr. Valencie noticed that the expenses of the household were becoming so large as to put his business at risk. He came to me to inform me of his worries. He was at a loss to understand where these bills came from. He had not seen you or your daughters dressing in anything particularly opulent and the household seemed to be running on the same lines as before. There no exotic meals. We had begun to investigate but had not got very far when, unfortunately, Mr. Valencie died.'

Gabriella began to feel the anger welling up in her. It seemed that her step-mother had made her father's last days particularly stressful. She paid particular attention.

'Then you, Madam,' the solicitor nodded to Mrs. Valencie, 'came to me with that new will. I suspected it was a forgery.'

'It most certainly was not,' Mrs. Valencie stated very loudly.

'But look at the position you are in, Madam. You do not seem to understand what has been discovered. I have set in motion some investigations which have produced results and I now know you owe a considerablc sum for gaming debts. Please do not deny it because I have discussed this matter with a certain man who I believe has called to your home on some occasions recently.'

Mrs. Valencie said nothing.

'So,' said the solicitor, 'the position is this. You, Mrs. Sertus, were never legally married to Mr. Valencie. It appears that you entered into this new marriage without the knowledge of what your first husband had done but, even so, the second marriage still was not legal.'

'I contest that and, believe me, I will find a solicitor who will make that marriage stand. I will find Mr. Sertus and will prosecute him for desertion.' Mrs. Valencie, now named Mrs. Sertus by the solicitor, almost jumped up and down on her seat.

'I do not think you will, Madam.' The solicitor waved some papers at her. 'You do not seem to understand your precarious situation. You see, I met with Mr. Sertus and offered him an alternative solution to his problem, which he accepted. Mr. Sertus wrote this affidavit on the promise that you would not prosecute him for his actions. In return, he would not prosecute you for fraud. Now, if you are prosecuted for fraud you would spend a long time in a debtors' prison and I am sure you will know that conditions in such places are less than desirable. In fact, they are dreadful, particularly in Grelland, which is where you would end up.'

Mrs. Sertus struggled for breath.

'Yes, indeed. Now, with regard to the problem of concern to us here today, I need to address the difficulty of the late Mr. Valencie's will. I believe, if I am able to arrange affairs so that the late Mr. Valencie's will benefits Miss Gabriella Valencie, that I can undertake on her behalf that she will not prosecute you for fraudulently making a false will.' The solicitor looked questioningly at Gabriella, who nodded.

'That will was not false. My husband made it properly and you said so when I brought it to you.' Mrs. Sertus's face was getting very red.

'I only stated it appeared to be in order. I knew it was not.'

Gabriella looked at the solicitor with the obvious question in her eyes, but the solicitor smiled and nodded to her as if to say he would answer everything later.

'Besides which, Mrs. Sertus, think of this. In that false will, everything was left to Mr. Valencie's 'dear wife'. That wife was not named, as I advised you at the time. You were never his dear wife. This means that Mr. Valencie left everything to his real wife, Miss Gabriella's mother. Now, under the terms of that lady's will, everything that made up her estate, even benefits which came to her after she died, was to be left to Miss Gabriella. So if that will you presented to me was good and true, then the first and only Mrs. Valencie inherits and she bequeaths everything to Miss Gabriella. Unfortunately I did not get around to including the names of the 'daughters' which were mentioned in the new will. Since Mrs. Valencie only had one daughter, only one daughter could inherit.'

'But that means I am left destitute. I have nothing. I looked after Gabriella for years and years. Am I now to be left with nothing, after all that work?' Mrs. Sertus was shedding angry tears.

James was so outraged he decided it was time he said something. 'But it was not you who did the work, was it, Madam? Gabriella has been doing the work as your servant for many months now. You have used her badly and I condemn your actions absolutely. You showed no concern for the person you thought to be your step-daughter. You did nothing to help the daughter of the man you used for your own ends. I cannot say enough against you.'

It was Gabriella turn to hold James's hand. 'Thank you,' she whispered, 'but look at what has been put right.' James conceded that something good had come out of it.

'Well, there may be a way out of all this,' said the solicitor. 'Under the terms of the will which I know to be good and true, your daughters, Mrs. Sertus, are provided for. They will not inherit such a great deal because you have depleted the amount of funds available but there will be a small amount which will be enough for your daughters to live upon. But there are conditions.

'Now, if Miss Gabriella agrees to the terms I have mentioned, I suggest the following: that you Mrs. Sertus, depart Essenia forthwith. I sent a letter yesterday to your daughter, Matilda, warning her that you will be coming to live with her for the foreseeable future. Again, if Miss Gabriella agrees, the last and proper will of Mr. Valencie will be validated. This will provide for your daughters. You, however, will not be provided for whatsoever. You will be totally dependent on your daughters.'

Mrs. Sertus made angry noises and struggled to find words to dispute the matter.

'It's that or the debtor's prison. Which do you prefer?' the solicitor asked.

Now Mrs. Sertus found her voice. 'I will return home now but you will hear from my lawyers as soon as I can contact them. I have been badly used. I am extremely angry with you especially, Gabriella. I still forbid any engagement.'

'Firstly, Mrs. Sertus, you cannot forbid anything. Mr. Valencie left me in control of Miss Gabriella's affairs,' the solicitor stated. 'You have no concern in this matter whatsoever. You still do not comprehend that you never were Miss Gabriella's step-mother.'

Mrs. Sertus got up from her chair and made as if to leave.

'Just a moment, Mrs. Sertus,' the solicitor stopped her. 'The second matter I have to deal with is that you are not to be allowed to return to the home you have lived in illegally for several years. In my outer office I have two guardsmen. These men have kindly provided a small carriage to transport you to Grelland this very day. Any belongings Miss Gabriella allows to be yours will be delivered in due course. Your housekeeper has packed a small valise for your immediate use. Your daughter Florence is waiting for you.'

Gabriella raised her eyes in surprise. The solicitor smiled kindly at her.

'You cannot use me like this,' Mrs. Sertus argued. 'I demand to speak to a lawyer today.'

The solicitor's patience was at an end. 'You may contact a lawyer when you reach Grelland but if you do not co-operate with our arrangements you will be arrested and will spend time in the guardhouse until your trial for forgery and fraud. Which is it to be?'

Mrs. Sertus said nothing.

'I thought so.' The solicitor got up, opened the door to his office and called his clerk. 'Mrs. Sertus is ready to leave now. And, Mrs. Sertus, I have an order here signed by the King that you are not to be allowed into Essenia ever again. In effect, you have been exiled. Let your own country deal with you.'

With that, Mrs. Sertus was swept out of the room by the guardsmen and taken out of the front door into the waiting carriage.

Chapter Twenty Seven

The solicitor turned back from the door and faced the two people left in his office. 'I believe we need some refreshments, yes?'

Gabriella sank back in her chair. 'If you please, Mr. Browning. I must admit to some little astonishment.'

'I can hardly believe it,' said James. 'It will take some time to get used to the new situation.'

'Indeed it will, Sir, but let me organise some tea.' The solicitor called for John.

While John disappeared into a back room the solicitor apologised for putting his young charge through the ordeal. 'I knew it would be difficult for you, Miss Gabriella. I needed you to be present while I informed that lady of her crimes so that you could agree to the terms I had decided upon. I can change them, of course, if, when you have had time to think about the matter, you decide you would prefer to prosecute Mrs. Sertus. I believe it would not be to your advantage though. It could cause you considerable anxiety and worry.'

'I understand,' said Gabriella. 'At this moment I do not believe there could have been a better arrangement than what has been decided upon. I do thank you for your help. I have one or two questions, of course.'

'Naturally, but let us stop for a moment to recover from the news.'

John re entered the room with a tray. He had found some

china cups in an old cupboard, washed them carefully and warmed them with hot water. He placed the tray before Gabriella and moved the handle of the teapot towards her right hand.

'Thank you,' she said but her hand shook so much that James took the teapot from her and poured the tea himself. He put a spoonful of sugar in Gabriella's cup and gave it to her.

'Have one of these macaroons too,' said James. 'They'll help with the shock.' He sought to divert Gabriella's mind from the morning's work. 'Did you get these from the baker's in the next road?' James enquired of John.

'Yes, Sir, I believe they are thought to be superior to the ones to be bought in the city.'

'Mm, very good,' replied James. But Gabriella's mind could not be diverted for long.

'May I ask what will happen if Mrs. Sertus does instruct a lawyer on her behalf? I would expect her to do something like that.'

'She may well do, but it would not be to her advantage,' said the solicitor. 'All that will happen is that the lawyer will send me a letter asking for information and I will send him a very long letter with all the information he could wish for and more. The lawyer will then explain to Mrs. Sertus that a legal battle would result in her possible imprisonment in the guardhouse. The King has only allowed Mrs. Sertus to be exiled if she does not cause any more problems. If she does not accept and comply with the terms of the exile she will be tried here for fraud.'

'May I ask a delicate question, Mr. Browning,' said Gabriella. 'I do not wish to be rude, but why did you not inform me that the new will was a forgery when you first got it?'

'Yes, I must apologise for that. I thought it the best course at the time. You see, Miss Gabriella, the law is somewhat unpredictable. I could have taken exception to that will immediately on reading it. But I had to consider what that course of action would result in.' The solicitor sipped his tea. 'All I had to go on at the time was that I believed Mr. Valencie's signature to be a forgery. If Mrs. Valencie had taken the matter to a judge, there was a chance she may have won the case and the new will would have become the standard. In that case, it would have been harder for me to counteract that judgement. I needed more information and a better legal basis for declaring the new will to be invalid before any matter came before a judge. So I had to pretend that I had sent the will to be recorded in the city. This kept Mrs. Valencie, as she was known, from using any money which had been invested on your behalf.'

Gabriella thought about it and nodded.

The solicitor put down his cup. 'You see, I did not want to give you any false hope. At the time I had nothing on which to base any hope, except a belief that I would find something wrong with Mrs. Valencie's affairs. I did not know then that things were so bad at your home. Fortunately the King relieved your working conditions a little but I must say that I am desolated you were made to work so hard. I was shocked also to discover that the money I sent for your allowance was being used for Mrs. Valencie's own ends. However, perhaps now we can make amends.'

'There is no need, thank you, Mr. Browning,' said Gabriella. 'You have been put to a great deal of trouble to help me and I must now find a way to pay you for your efforts. If you would be good enough to send me an account, I will find a way to reimburse you as soon as I can.'

'That will not be necessary, Miss Gabriella. Your sentiments are much appreciated, but your father left matters completely in my hands and I have been compensated for my work. Perhaps now would be a good time to show you the records of your father's investments. If you would excuse me I will fetch them.'

James and Gabriella were very quiet for a moment. 'This has been quite a surprise for you, Gabriella,' James said as he took her hand.

Gabriella held tightly to James. 'Yes, but in a good way. I expect it will take some time before I realise exactly how the changes will affect me but at present the future is a lot brighter than it was this morning.' She smiled at James who kissed her hand. 'I feel a little overwhelmed with all the new things to take into consideration but I will get used to it.'

'I believe this may have solved your difficulties with regard to our marriage. I do not believe Mrs. Valencie, sorry, Mrs. Sertus, now can make any credible accusations about your father.'

'I cannot think of a situation whereby she could spread rumours but I have underestimated my former step-mother before. She may think of something to take revenge on us. But I can leave that problem for a month or two and concentrate on how this news will change my life. Oh, I forgot Nanny. She will be wondering what has happened.'

The solicitor returned with a large folder and set it on the desk. 'I think you may have had enough to deal with this morning, Miss Gabriella, so I propose to give you this statement of your accounts which you can peruse at your leisure. Come back to me next week and I will explain everything. You have been well provided for despite the inroads Mrs. Sertus made on your father's affairs. It's not as much as your father would have liked but it is substantial enough.'

* * *

James walked Gabriella home and they grandly entered by the front door.

'It's wonderful for us to be able to do this and not to have to hide anymore,' said James.

'Yes, thank you, James. I hope to be able to welcome you with better hospitality from now on. I expect there would be some lunch ready if you would like to stay.'

'I would love to stay but the Queen will be anxious to know the news and I know Nanny needs to have you to herself today. I will call tomorrow morning, if I may.'

So Gabriella waved goodbye to James secure in the knowledge that tomorrow would be the start of a happier time for them both. She ran to the kitchen where Nanny was stirring a pot of soup. The kitchen table was laid for three.

'There you are, dear,' said Nanny. 'Come and have some soup. Susie and Bob have already eaten theirs. I expect you have some news. Am I allowed to know what it is?'

'Of course you are, Nanny. But first tell me what happened here this morning.'

'It was most unusual. Mrs. Valencie went out, as you know. Shortly after that, there was a loud knock on the door. I thought at first it was that man who comes to visit Mrs. Valencie. But it was the Captain of the Guard. I was most surprised. Anyway, he came in and asked me to pack a bag for Mrs. Valencie and another for Florence. Well, I was unsure what to do without orders from you but the Captain said the King had given orders for it to be done and you'd be grateful if I did as he wanted. So that's what I did. I couldn't see any harm in it. I hope I did the right thing.'

'Yes, you did, thank you, but what happened with Florence?'

'I was told to help her get ready. She was to accompany the Captain to where they would meet Mrs. Valencie. There was a maidservant in the carriage waiting to look after Miss Florence on the short journey, so I did not worry too much. I found it very hard to understand what was happening, but I was wondering if Mrs. Valencie was going to visit Miss Matilda.'

'Yes, that's where she has gone.'

'Will she be back soon?'

'No, Nanny, but I think I had better tell you the whole story. Eat something with me first and I'll tell you. Mr. Georges might like to hear this too, if you want to call him.'

* * *

The old couple sat quietly while Gabriella explained the new circumstances.

'We are so pleased for you, child. There can be nothing to prevent your marriage now.' Nanny pulled a handkerchief out of her pocket and blew her nose.

'You must be wondering what will become of the two of you,' Gabriella said gently.

'I was thinking of that, Miss,' said Mr. Georges forlornly. 'But I expect we will find some situation to suit us.'

'No, you won't,' said Gabriella with a smile. 'You are to come with me to the Palace, if you want. James says there is a cottage in the grounds of the Palace which you may like or there is a small apartment. You are to retire, although the Queen asked if you would be kind enough to advise her with regard to jam-making, Nanny.'

Nanny laughed with relief and looked at her husband, who nodded his head gently, obviously pleased.

'Or if you prefer, you can stay here in this house. It is completely up to you what you decide to do. You have worked hard all your lives and taken such good care of me. Take some time to think about what you want to do. There is no need to decide immediately. However, what I would like you to do soon is move into the front room upstairs. You have lived for far too long in that back room down here.'

'We could not do that, Gabriella,' Nanny objected. 'You should have that room.'

'I'm very happy in my own room. I do not want to move my things now, and then again when I go to the Palace. Still, there is no need for us to do anything quickly, so we can take our time.'

Nanny and Mr. George looked bemused but happy. Nanny hugged Gabriella tightly. And for the first time in two years Gabriella thought that at last she could allow herself to believe that happiness with James was possible.

Chapter Twenty Eight

Mrs. Sertus sat in the carriage in silence. Florence had tried to ask some questions but Mrs. Sertus had looked so angry that Florence leant back in her seat and kept quiet.

After travelling for an hour they stopped at a roadside inn to take some refreshment. Mrs. Valencie drank a little coffee but refused all food. Florence was hungry but did not like to eat too much. She was afraid her mother would not look kindly on a good appetite. So both women climbed back into the carriage less than happy.

It was dark when they reached Matilda's home and the place did not look inviting at all. The old housekeeper opened the door to them and asked them into the drawing room where a cold supper was laid out. Matilda came to meet them as she heard them come in. Florence was so hungry that she sat at the small table to eat regardless of her mother's opinion. But she kept quiet.

Matilda, however, was full of questions. 'I am pleased to see you, of course, Mama, but why are you here? I got a letter saying you were coming but I could not understand why you had to come so quickly and without me being able to make proper arrangements. The housekeeper has made up some beds but the rooms are not as comfortable as I would like. Things are not so good here after all. Have some tea, Mama. It will help you after your journey, but please tell me what is happening. Is Gabriella coming too?'

Mrs. Sertus shuddered. 'Don't mention that girl's name, if you please. I am so upset I cannot say anything now. I am so tired. Maybe tomorrow I can tell you something.'

'Very well, Mama. Let me take you to your room and you can rest. I'll bring this cup of tea for you.' Matilda took her mother away but returned soon to see if Florence could tell her anything.

'I don't know anything, Sis,' said Florence. 'I've been trying to get to the bottom of this all day but Mama was in such a bad mood that I daren't keep asking. You'll have to wait, sorry. All I can tell you is that I was rudely awakened this morning by Nanny who told me I had to get up and get ready to go out. And I have ended up here. I don't know what is going on.'

* * *

The next morning Mrs. Sertus arose late. She looked a little recovered from the journey and was glad to eat some bread and butter for breakfast with her cup of tea. But her face still was set in an angry frown as it had been the previous evening.

'Do you feel well enough to inform me of what is happening, Mama,' Matilda enquired. 'I need to make some arrangements for your visit. How long will you be staying, do you think?'

'Did not that letter inform you that I am here to live with you for the rest of my life?'

Matilda gasped. 'I don't understand. What is to become of your home in Essenia?'

'That ungrateful girl has thrown me out.'

'But Gabriella could not do such a thing. I thought the new will stipulated that everything was left to you.'

'Gabriella has cheated me out of my home. She always wanted everything for herself and now she has done it but only by deceit. She was always jealous of us. She did not want your step-father to love us as he did and now she has found an excuse to get rid of us. After everything I did for her and all the hard work I had to do to take care of her, this is what happens. She managed to get that dreadful solicitor to say that the new will was a forgery. So she got everything and turned us out of the house as quickly as she could.'

'But the letter I got two days ago wrote that you are here by order of the King. What did the King have to do with all this? I still don't understand how this could have happened.' Matilda fussed about with the teapot and poured herself more tea.

But Mrs. Sertus relapsed into silence.

Matilda gave up waiting for answers. 'I don't know if I can keep you here. There is so little money. I have my own problems. Roland has gone away and I do not know when he will be back. I don't know how we are to manage.'

'There is another letter for you from the solicitor. I don't know what is in it, but read it. I expect it is more bad news.' Mrs. Sertus took a letter out of her purse and gave it to Matilda, who grabbed it and opened it quickly. 'Well?' asked Mrs. Sertus after a while.

'Things may not be so bad,' said Matilda slowly. 'The old will made provision for me and Florence. We will both get a small allowance. It's a help anyway. But listen,' Matilda lowered her voice, 'I don't want Roland to know of this. I think he wastes money and if he finds out about my allowance I am sure he will demand it for himself. I need it to manage the household. It's better if he doesn't know there is a little coming in.'

'You would have got far more under the new will,' said Mrs. Sertus. 'Gabriella made sure you did not get what is yours by rights.'

'Mama, you were the one who got everything under the

new will. Florence and I saw very little of it, as I remember. It was Gabriella who bought me some essential things for my wedding. You said you were unable to buy me those. I do find it hard to see how I benefitted from the new will. According to this letter from the solicitor, under the old will I will have enough to buy myself essential clothes.'

'Maybe you could help me with some of it, Matilda,' Mrs. Sertus suggested.

'I don't think there will be enough,' said Matilda. 'I will have to use most of it to buy household things, at least until Roland comes back. Even when Roland comes back I do not believe he will give me much for the household bills, if he gives me anything at all. Perhaps Florence will give you some after she has helped me with the expense of keeping you here.'

But Florence looked mutinous. 'I don't know how much there will be and I don't know what my future holds so I expect I will have to save a lot of it.'

The three ladies continued to bicker until the housekeeper asked if she could clear the table.

* * *

Roland, meanwhile, had burnt off his bad temper by attending the races with a friend. He gambled what money he had and lost it all, but he did not care. He knew he would have to return home and sell his new carriage. He wondered how his bride was coping with the old house and no comforts. He hoped it would be a lesson to her.

He still had not decided what to do with Matilda. He saw little beyond a divorce. He hoped to keep the divorce as quiet as possible, but the only bride he wished for in exchange knew all about the wedding and its consequences. He still harboured designs on Essenia's gold and had not given up on his plans. A new one began to form in his mind, to which he needed to give some thought.

For the present he had no choice but to face the problems waiting for him at home.

Chapter Twenty Nine

From that time on, James was able to visit Gabriella every day. He had given himself leave to defer his working life in order to devote time to Gabriella.

The weather conspired to give these days of courtship much pleasure. James and Gabriella were able to drive out in a carriage in warm sunshine. Nanny accompanied them often, sometimes looking for wild strawberries or blueberries while her charges wandered ahead of her. Occasionally Mr. Georges joined the party and dozed in the carriage while the young couple strolled nearby.

The couple's love for each other deepened as each day went by. James delighted in Gabriella's strength of character, her devotion to her housekeeper and her loyalty to himself, regardless of danger. Gabriella loved James's capable handling of his duties, his intelligent plans for the country and, above all else, his constancy in loving her.

The Queen renewed her invitation to Jemima to come to the ball. She included with it a long letter of news from the Palace. Jemima was pleased to read that Prince James had become engaged. She sent a letter back to the Queen with an invitation of her own. Jemima's brother had asked if Prince James and his fiancé would enjoy a visit with his family in Farren. He knew of the friendship between Jemima and James's friend Peter and wished to give her every opportunity to develop it. Believing that Jemima would one day live in Essenia her brother kindly acted to help her make friends in advance. Jemima mentioned in her letter that she would engage a maid to help in the household while Jemima entertained her guests.

So before long, James and Gabriella set off for Farren, taking along one of the old cook's nieces, who was to help temporarily. The initial shyness between Gabriella and Jemima soon disappeared as they became acquainted. Neither girl had had an easy life but each had dealt as well as possible with the difficulties while keeping a sense of the ridiculous. Gabriella's life had been the harder so she was quieter than Jemima but both were eager to take a full part in whatever activity was suggested.

So they played frenetic games of badminton, improvised a bowling green on the lawn (much to the disgust of the gardener), walked along the nearby seashore and each evening discussed the thorny problems associated with topics ranging from estate management to the care of kittens. Jemima's brother entertained them with stories of his travels, while her mother smiled on them from a comfortable armchair.

On one of their walks, Jemima asked James and Gabriella where they would live once they were married.

'We are to have an apartment in the Palace,' James said. 'There is a set of rooms in the south wing which has not been used for many years. The rooms are light and airy, with windows looking over the lake. We will need new furnishings, which I hope Gabriella will decide upon soon.'

'We will not need very much. There is quite a lot of furniture already in the apartment. All we need do is take off the dust covers. We will take our meals with the King and Queen, who like company,' Gabriella explained. 'I would like to help the Queen with the cooking arrangements, although she says she is not bringing me to the Palace to do her work. I will have to find something to do so I am hoping the gardener will allow me some ground to grow herbs. My elderly servants taught me how to grow things and I found I enjoyed being out in the garden.'

'It sounds lovely,' said Jemima wistfully.

'Will you be coming to live in Essenia shortly?' asked James.

'It is not possible at present,' said Jemima. 'Peter does not believe it will be suitable for us to live with his parents. I agree with him, but it will be hard for us to find somewhere to live within our limited circumstances.' But it was not in Jemima's character to be unhappy. 'Everything will work out well, I am sure.'

One morning, while Jemima attended to some household matters, James and Gabriella had time to themselves to walk in the family's extensive grounds. James tucked Gabriella's hand firmly under his arm.

'Jemima has a lovely home, James, don't you think? But I do prefer our lake.'

James looked around him. 'The scenery is pretty here, I'll allow, but a little tame for our northern tastes. It's beautiful, but in a different way.'

James took Gabriella to a seat in a small arbour. 'Gabriella, I want to ask you if you are sure you can cope with the small amount of income at the Palace. I am trying to improve the situation but it will take time. The jam-making has had surprising results. I found the Queen a small warehouse where we set up new cooking stoves and tables. We engaged some staff and taught them how to make the jam and, although there is room for improvement, we believe it will be a good business eventually. The treasury found us some funding which helped immensely. So this year should be profitable. There will be plenty of fruit. The Secretary asked farmers to grow as much as they could. We are going to sell the jam to some merchants in Farren and Grelland. Even so, the income will not be large, especially at first.'

'James, dearest, I have some income of my own if I want anything extra. But I cannot think of anything I would need. I learnt how to manage on little and it helped me realise that it is people who matter, not whether I have a good dining table or silk drapes. Some things are necessary but I can manage with simple things and be happy.'

'Our circumstances have changed, haven't they? At first you were worried about not having a dowry and now I am the one to worry that I will not be able to give you the sort of life you would have if you remained in your own house.'

'James, I went from having a large room of my own, elaborate chairs to sit on and expensive clothing, to sleeping in the kitchen, wearing old aprons and sitting on a hard bench. But while I had all the good things, my father was often away. So I had to sit with my step-mother and sisters and was so unhappy. When my life changed and I lived in the kitchen, I had a lot of love and kindness from Nanny. I was far happier.' Gabriella paused. 'I put cushions on the bench!'

James laughed. 'That was a very serious speech.'

'Yes, wasn't it? Do you think Jemima would be shocked if later I asked to paddle in the sea?'

'She would be the first to suggest it.'

When the visit came to an end, Jemima's brother was pleased to know that Jemima was to travel with her new friends to attend the Queen's ball.

The only thing which detracted from James's enjoyment was the knowledge that he had yet to deal with the threat from Roland. But he was able to put it to the back of his mind, deciding he would make arrangements to deal with it when he returned to Essenia.

Chapter Thirty

One warm morning at the beginning of July, the Captain of the Guard and Sam Smithick entered the Palace gates and knocked on the door. Jenny let them in and directed them to the Library where the King was waiting for them with James and Mr. Secretary.

'Good morning,' said the King. 'We are pleased to see you. The maids will bring some refreshment later but, if we may, we'll get down to business.'

'Of course, Sir,' said the Captain and sat down beside the King's desk. Sam was inclined to remain standing but James offered him a chair by the window.

'Now, what plans do we have for this dangerous situation at the forthcoming ball?' asked the King.

'The plans are yet to be perfected but I will outline what we have decided so far and see if we can improve on them.' The Captain took some notes out of a pocket. 'The main plan is to dress young Smithick in the same clothes as Prince James and hide him in a suitable position so that, when the time comes, the assailants will believe he is the Prince. We suspect that the Prince will receive a message in which he will be asked to step outside for a moment. We believe the best place for an abduction to take place is at one of the back entrances to the ballroom. The one nearest the road seems most likely. If we hide Smithick at that entrance, we can substitute him for the Prince as he steps out of the door.'

'But that puts Sam at risk and I would not be comfortable with such a plan,' said James with concern.

'He is unlikely to come to any harm, Sir. If you remember, the plan of Sir Roland's servants was simply to capture you and take you away elsewhere to, er, dispose of you. So we will hide several guardsmen outside that entrance who will jump out as soon as the assailants emerge and capture them. We believe Smithick will be able to get into the open before he is attacked, which will give our other guardsmen the opportunity to prevent any serious harm.'

'Is there anywhere to hide there?' asked the King.

'There are several bushes, Sir, and we would like to request some other things, perhaps a few packing trunks or the like to hide our men.'

The mention of bushes brought a few memories to mind for James and he had to hide a grin. James would always associate bushes with guardsmen and wondered if, in future, he would be able to pass one without looking behind it.

'We also suggest that we place a few guardsmen in the ballroom dressed as guests,' the Captain continued. 'They can protect the Prince should there be any direct attack. This seems unlikely but we would like to be prepared for any eventuality.'

'What happens if things do not go to plan?' asked the King. 'For example, suppose James is asked to go out of a different doorway?'

'We thought the Prince would be able to give a message to one of the guardsmen in the ballroom to the effect that the plan had changed. These men then could go outside and warn Smithick and the hidden men to go to the other destination. We would need to set up hiding places at each place. It's cumbersome, I know, Sir, but I think it is workable. What we would like to do is arrange a dress rehearsal to see what problems we encounter.'

'That sounds sensible. What do you think, Mr. Secretary?'

'Yes, it seems a very good plan. But can we keep everything as secret as possible? At present Roland does not believe we know of his plans, so the element of surprise is with us. The more people involved in this plan the more danger there is of something leaking out, which could get back to Roland's servants.'

'It is a danger, of course,' said the Captain. 'I believe six men would suffice in the ballroom and another six hidden in the garden. We can place others openly at the main gate to the Palace and they would not need necessarily to be informed of the plans, although I would like to warn them on the night of a possible need for action. I have more than twelve men whom I trust implicitly; good-living men who are in no danger of getting drunk and so on.'

'It would be necessary for the Prince to stay in the ballroom at all times other than to comply with the abduction plan, unless he were to be accompanied by two guardsmen,' said Mr. Secretary. 'I understand the Prince likes to help the Queen with preparations in the kitchen, but we have engaged the cook's niece and others to help instead.'

'That is important, James,' said the King. 'We need to know where you are at all times.'

'Yes, thank you, Sir,' said James. 'But what about Gabriella? Is she to be protected too?'

'Of course, Sir, although we do not think she is in such danger, there being no plans that we know of, or could imagine, to harm her now that Sir Roland is married. However, we will place two competent guardsmen to look after her. She is always accompanied by her housekeeper if she ventures out these days. I, myself, would think twice before I tried to come between that lady and Miss Gabriella to do any harm.'

James smiled. 'That's true enough.'

* * *

In the next two weeks there was a flurry of activity at the Palace. The Captain of the Guard chose six men who knew how to dance and how to behave in polite society. Six others were chosen who would be strong enough to deal with the ruffians who had designs on the Prince. They were given instructions to arrest those criminals. Roland was to be captured too, as soon as it became clear he was involved in the planned abduction. All twelve guardsmen came to the Palace under the pretext of arranging furniture for the Queen's ball.

The furniture was arranged, but it was done to keep doorways clear in case the guardsmen needed to run out quickly.

Some of the plans worked and others did not. Jenny and Nell were asked to dance with two of the guardsmen, but it was discovered that it would be impossible for the men to leave their fair partners in the middle of a dance. So these men were asked to dress as footmen instead of guests. If any of the guests asked them to do something, they were to pass the instructions on to the real servants and to resume their careful observation of the Prince.

They practiced changing the door at which the Prince was to leave. The Captain whispered to James the location of the way out to be tested. James passed the information on to the guardsman nearest to him, who left the ballroom by a different door, ran around to Sam and the others in hiding and got them to run to the new entrance. There was a lot of confusion at first, with some guardsmen running in the wrong direction, but once the men got to know the Palace doors better, the plan worked well.

Mr. Secretary said he would find costumes for the guardsmen who were to be footmen. He knew of households who would be able to lend uniforms. These kind people would expect the King to engage extra servants for the ball, so it would not produce any talk.

At times a lot of laughter could be heard coming from James's dressing room as Sam tried to copy James's costume. 'No, that's not right,' James was heard to say several times. 'Like this.' In the end they managed to make Sam look something like the Prince. The Captain thought Sam needed some dark powder on his hair but Sam objected, saying that there would be little enough daylight on the night of the ball and his hat would cover his fairer hair.

Chapter Thirty One

Roland returned home one evening having spent all his money. His wife welcomed him warily. She enquired as to his health and asked if he had dined as she had already eaten. Roland told her shortly that he would find himself something in the kitchen, but Matilda went before him and brought out what food was left over in the pantry.

She set a loaf of bread, some cold meat and a small salad on the dining room table.

'I have little to offer you, I'm afraid,' said Matilda. 'There is some fruit cake too, if you would like some later. Tomorrow I will prepare a better meal for you, although my resources are limited as I am sure you are aware. Please eat. I will go to see if there is some ale in the cellar. None of us likes it.'

Roland had sat at the table in a bad humour but looked up at that. 'Us? Surely you do not offer ale to the housekeeper.'

'Oh, maybe you do not know, but my mother and sister are here.'

Roland stiffened. 'What? Visiting so soon? I did not expect to see them for at least another month or two.'

'They are not here to visit,' said Matilda defensively. 'They are going to live with us.'

Roland exploded. 'No, they cannot. I told you I was going to institute a divorce. There will be nowhere for you to live, let alone your family. You must tell them to leave in the morning and you can go with them.' He threw a slice of bread back onto his plate and pushed it away. 'You must go back to your house in Essenia. I will make the arrangements now.' Roland got up out of his seat and prepared to go out to the stables.

'Wait a minute, Sir,' said Matilda. 'That will not be possible and under no circumstances am I leaving here tomorrow. You may go, if you wish, but this is my rightful home and I am staying in it.'

'What do you mean when you say it's not possible for your family to leave?'

'Sit down, Roland. It's a long story and you need to know the circumstances. But I warn you now that I am not leaving here. I have consulted your solicitor and I am within my rights to stay here and there is nothing you can do about that at present.'

'We'll see about that. You seem to have been busy. What else have you done that I should know about?'

Matilda ignored his last comment. 'My mother has been turned out of her house by my step-sister. Gabriella managed to get my step-father's will declared void, which means that the house and all the money belong to Gabriella and not my mother as we previously thought. It appears that Gabriella also has been able to get an order from the King to exile my mother. This means, of course, that my mother is not allowed to stay in Essenia. It is a grave injustice and we are considering what we can do about it but, as you must know, an order from the King is not easy to overturn. At present there is nowhere else for my mother and sister to go.'

Matilda did not inform Roland that recently she had received a letter forwarded to her by Gabriella. This letter had been from one of her mother's creditors demanding payment of debts of honour. The letter had stated that since the sender had been informed of Mrs. Valencie's daughter's recent marriage, it appeared the said daughter would now be in a position to pay the debts mentioned. Matilda had been horrified and had confronted her mother with the news.

There had been a terrible row culminating in Mrs. Sertus locking herself into her room and Matilda flouncing out into the garden to walk about trying to decide what to do about matters.

Matilda, after some thought, had decided that the creditor did not appear to know her mother's whereabouts, since the letter had been sent to their former home in Essenia. Also her mother now had a different name so it would give Matilda some time in order to visit the solicitor once more to determine what could be done to prevent Matilda being liable for her mother's debts.

But Matilda had more pressing problems, the most immediate being to convince Roland that there was nothing he could do to turn her out of her home.

'I believe there is little we can accomplish at this late hour. I suggest we retire for the night and discuss the matter more calmly tomorrow. Your room is ready for you.' With that Matilda stood up and left the room, leaving Roland to sulk alone.

* * *

The following morning Roland was up early. He went to look at his carriage to decide where best he could sell it. His anger at finding it already sold knew no bounds and he stormed into the house telling the housekeeper to find his wife immediately and bring her to the library.

The housekeeper told him that his wife had already left the house and had gone to the market. He would probably find her there if he did not want to wait until she returned. Or, she informed him, his sister and mother-in-law would be down shortly if he wished to take breakfast with them.

Roland turned on his heels, grabbed a cloak from his room and left the house banging the door behind him. He had no wish to air his grievances with his wife in public so he thought the best use of his time would be to visit his solicitor in order to start divorce proceedings. He strode into the solicitor's office. Unfortunately the clerk explained he would have to wait for about an hour as the solicitor was already speaking to another client. Roland said he would come back the next day.

Roland caught up with Matilda on her way home. 'I want the money you got by selling my carriage,' he stated shortly. 'What made you think you could come to my home, steal my belongings and sell them?'

'What made you believe you could leave me here in this place without any money to buy what was needed just to exist?' Matilda replied angrily.

They argued all the way home, neither giving way to the other. Roland left Matilda at the front door while he strode around the house to the old stables. He knew it was futile but there might have been some other things which he could sell. Roland soon realised Matilda had arranged matters so that there was food to eat, but Roland did not consider food to be a priority.

The next few days were uncomfortable. Roland treated his mother-in-law with disdain so dinner time was fraught with sarcastic comments. Soon though Roland began to look at his situation differently and wondered if he could use it to his own advantage. The dinner table became quieter as Roland worked out his plans.

* * *

Roland entered the breakfast room one morning to tell the ladies he knew who their princess was.

'Which princess?' asked Florence.

'The one you said was seen with Prince James.'

'Oh, do you really know? Who is it?' Florence stopped eating her toast.

'Your step-sister, Miss Gabriella.'

Matilda nearly dropped her tea cup. 'No, it cannot be Gabriella. We would have known if she had been walking out with the Prince.'

'What makes you think it is my step-daughter, Sir?' asked Mrs. Sertus coldly.

'I have it on good authority,' he said. He then ignored his companions and filled a plate with eggs.

'Which good authority do you mean, Roland?' asked Matilda.

'You do not wish to believe me so I see no point in telling you.'

'Oh, please do,' said Florence.

'If you must know, I met some people on my travels who had been given reliable information in Essenia. It seems the Prince had been followed by a guardsman who had witnessed Prince James putting a ring on Miss Gabriella's finger. Apparently the guardsman was so overjoyed that he could not contain himself and whispered the matter to a friend. Soon everyone in Essenia knew the Prince was engaged.'

It had been a shock for Roland to discover the matter, and he had nearly given up on his plans. But on reflection he decided it was unlikely an announcement concerning the engagement would be made before the ball, which meant he still had time to carry out his plan. It was cutting things fine but Roland liked the excitement engendered by the risk. His arrogance made him believe he could achieve his ends; that his audaciousness would take everyone by surprise and ensure success.

'How could it possibly be Gabriella?' asked Matilda. 'She was always at home.'

'There was that time she went with Nanny to help at the Palace,' said Florence.

'Yes, I know, but she was to spend the day in the kitchens.'

'Maybe she did not,' said Roland.

'That wicked girl,' exclaimed Mrs. Sertus. 'She told me she would do all the work Nanny could not. She should not have had time to do anything else. If I had known what she was doing I would have put a stop to her outings straight away. It must have been after that girl, Susie, came. If I remember rightly Gabriella spent a lot of time going to the market after that.'

'Surely you must have known, Mama, if Gabriella was to be engaged to the Prince,' said Matilda.

'On the day I was wrongly evicted from my home I was given to understand Gabriella was engaged to someone. I could not be sure it was the Prince. I objected to any engagement, of course, but was overruled. No good will come of it, mark my words.'

'Overruled by whom, Mama? And why did you not tell us?' Mrs. Sertus did not answer.

'And where would Gabriella get good clothes from?' objected Matilda. 'The stories we heard were that the princess wore very expensive clothes. Gabriella had nothing like that. I know because I looked.'

'You looked?' asked Florence.

'Yes, and so did you, so don't pretend to be so virtuous,' said Matilda. 'All Gabriella's clothes were old. She didn't need anything else.'

'Maybe the Queen gave her some,' said Florence.

'I suppose the Queen might have some clothes left over from her younger days, but it seems unlikely to me.'

Roland finished his breakfast and left the ladies to their quarrels. He had more plans to make, although he thought he had just set some things in motion which would be of help to him later.

Chapter Thirty Two

There was little for Gabriella to do to get ready for the ball. She helped the Queen with some flower decorations, but everything else was organised by the Queen who left a lot of the cooking to the staff engaged for the occasion.

Gabriella had already collected her new shoes from the shoemaker. They were made of the softest white leather and fitted perfectly. Small silver buckles had been attached above the toes. The old shoemaker had polished them to such an extent that Gabriella thought she could see her reflection in them.

So on the day of the ball Nanny brushed Gabriella's long dark tresses until they shone, pinned her hair up in an intricate knot but allowed some tendrils to escape to frame her face.

'Lovely,' said Nanny when Gabriella presented herself for inspection. 'Your mother would be so proud of you, dear. Now, take a shawl with you too. It may be cooler when you come home. I'll be waiting for you.'

'I'll wear the shawl the Queen gave me as an engagement present. Up until now I had to hide it from my step-sisters. Please do not wait up,' said Gabriella. 'I will be very late and you need some sleep. The Queen will make sure I get home safely.'

'Very well, dear. So, go and enjoy your evening. I believe William Gilbert is waiting for you outside with the carriage.'

Gabriella entered the ballroom to be greeted by the King, Queen and Prince James. As soon as Gabriella arrived, James was allowed to leave his post and accompany her into the main room. It was full of light, both from the setting sun and a lot of candles set high above the guests. A band of musicians was playing quietly and already the room was crowded.

'It's wonderful, James,' said Gabriella. 'Where did you get all these candles?'

'My uncle sent them, along with several cases of wine, so there should be plenty of merriment. My uncle would like to say hello to you, and then we can dance a little, if you please.'

'Of course I must speak to your uncle. I have not talked to him for a long time. But look, James, is that Roland over there? Did Matilda come with him?'

'Yes, we couldn't prevent him coming as he had already received his invitation long ago. Matilda and Florence are together at the side of the room, by one of your flower arrangements. We can avoid them for now, if you don't mind.'

'Of course, but I will have to speak to Matilda before too long. It will look odd if I do not and will set people talking.'

They picked their way over to James's uncle stopping often as other guests greeted them. James's uncle was speaking to Peter and Jemima. Gabriella was delighted to be reunited with her friends, which made her feel very much more comfortable in the crowd.

The uncle marvelled at how beautiful all the young ladies looked. 'I'm going to sit here now, my dears, and watch you young people dance.' So James and Peter took Gabriella and Jemima and made up a set for the next dance.

'Don't step on my feet as you pass,' said Peter to James.

'I dance as well as you do,' retorted James.

'That's what I am worried about.'

The girls called them to order. James and Peter were less

than elegant but they all enjoyed themselves greatly as the girls at least twirled prettily around the room.

So the evening passed pleasantly. Roland came over once to ask Gabriella to dance with him but she was able to apologise and excuse herself in that it was time for some refreshments and she and James were to lead the guests into the dining room. For the rest of the evening James manoeuvred things so that Gabriella was nowhere near Roland. He checked frequently with the 'footmen' as to the whereabouts of Roland's servants.

Towards the end of the evening James began to believe that Roland had changed his plans. James had received no message to ask him to leave the ballroom. He thought maybe Roland was going to abduct him from his bed or before breakfast the next day.

James was discussing this quietly with Mr. Secretary while Gabriella danced with a shy young man who had begged for the honour. Then one of the serving girls came to him to say that Miss Gabriella was feeling a little faint and would the Prince kindly attend her. She said Miss Gabriella was waiting by the front door in order to get a little air.

'I'll come immediately. Is she being cared for?'

'Yes, Sir, I believe Miss Florence is with her.'

James walked quickly to the front door but there was no sign of Gabriella. Another serving girl approached and asked if he was looking for Miss Gabriella.

'She was feeling very unwell, Sir, so she ordered the carriage and is now sitting in it waiting to see you before she goes.'

James immediately suspected foul play but he could not risk waiting for any of the guards to come with him in case Gabriella was really ill. The carriage was the one from the Palace stables so it appeared that Gabriella had certainly ordered it. James could not see anyone attending to the horses but he supposed that William Gilbert was looking after Gabriella's safety. He hurried down the steps to the gate.

Suddenly several things happened at once. The carriage set off up the road and gathered speed quickly. Another carriage drew up to the Palace gates and two men got down and rushed towards the Prince. But James heard a shout from the side wall of the Palace.

'I'm coming, Sir. Don't let them take you.' And with that Sam rushed towards him, followed by several other guardsmen. The two men from the carriage, who James now saw were Roland's servants, turned tail and ran towards the carriage. James ran after them and managed to trip one up. Sam issued loud orders to his men to catch the ruffians before they escaped. One had managed to get to the carriage and was climbing up to the driving seat, but Sam caught his foot and pulled hard. The man fell to the ground with a crunch. Sam left him to be captured by the others and rushed back to the Prince's side.

'Are you hurt, Sir?'

'No, but bring two of your men and follow me. Quickly now.'

James ran back up the Palace steps into the ballroom while Sam issued further orders. He called two of the guardsmen to him. 'Search the room for Miss Gabriella, please, and ask the Queen if she has seen her. I need you to be as fast as you can, but try not to upset the guests.'

James surveyed the room but could not see Gabriella anywhere. However, he did see Matilda sitting by an open window and walked over to her.

'Have you seen Gabriella in the last few minutes?' he asked.

'No,' Matilda answered tersely.

'There is a possibility that your husband has taken Gabriella away in a carriage. Do you know where he is likely to go?' James was getting angrier by the minute.

'Taken Gabriella? Why would he want to do such a thing?' James could see that she was genuinely surprised.

'Is Miss Florence nearby? Maybe she knows.'

'I don't know where she is. She told me she wanted some air and that was about half an hour ago.'

James quickly walked back to the front door trying to smile as he passed curious guests. Sam was waiting for him.

At that moment William Gilbert appeared at the bottom of the Palace steps. He had a large cut on his face. James ran down to him. 'What happened to you?' he said.

'They tied me up, Sir, and went off with the carriage,' said William indignantly. 'It took me all this time to get free. What do you want me to do now, Sir? Let me help as I can, please.'

'Yes, get my horse ready for me and take these guardsmen with you who will also need horses. Very quickly please.' James turned to Sam. 'Go with William now and come back with the horses. We're chasing after that carriage. I suspect Roland is driving it. I'll inform Mr. Secretary while you do that.'

By that time the Captain of the Guard had appeared around the side of the Palace and was waiting by the gate. James beckoned to him and ran to meet him. 'If you please, Captain, in a moment I would like you to take this other carriage and follow me. With your permission I'll take Sam and two others.'

'Will you be safe, Sir?'

'Yes. I'm not staying behind.'

By the time the horses were ready and William had brought them to the Palace gates, the two guardsmen had returned.

'I couldn't find Miss Valencie anywhere in the ballroom, Sir,' said one. 'We couldn't find Sir Roland either.'

'And the Queen told one of the maids to look upstairs but Miss Valencie is nowhere to be found, sorry,' said the other.

'The Queen sent this coat for you, Sir, and begs you will be careful.'

James clenched his hands in worry. 'I need one more coat if we can find one quickly,' he said. One of the guardsmen took his coat off and offered it to the Prince.

'Good,' said James pleased. He hurried to the horses and handed the coat to Sam who was already mounted. 'Put it on. We won't last with just court clothes on. Let's go. We'll keep to the road to Grelland mostly. If we think it is possible the carriage took a side road we'll look for tracks, although they will be hard to find in this dry weather.'

With that they set off at a fast pace. After half an hour they stopped to look down a side lane but James could see no sign of any recent travellers. 'We're wasting time,' he said urgently. 'Back to the main road.'

They urged their horses onwards. James wondered how long his men would keep up this pace. They had already had a long day and would need to rest soon. If necessary, he would travel on alone but it was not something he wanted to contemplate.

The party stopped to look along a side road which led back to Farren. Although James thought it unlikely Roland would take such a detour he could not ignore the possibility. But it was evident there were no signs of Roland on that road.

They stopped again at the road to a small port. There was only one port in Essenia. The village which served this port was built to accommodate fishermen and merchants with small businesses. Most merchants preferred to use the larger port in Grelland but small cargo boats could land at Essenia's port.

Once again James did not believe Roland had any reason to take this road but he had to look to make sure. He was worried about the time all this searching was taking. James and Sam left the rest of the men at the end of the road and, leading their horses, went on foot to search for tracks.

Impatiently James ran down the road but, despite looking carefully at the foot of hedges, could find nothing to suggest a carriage had driven this way.

'Sam, there's nothing here. Let's go back.'

Sam was on the other side of the road. 'Just a moment, Sir. I may have found something.' He handed James a scruffy object covered in dust.

'Ah, no,' said James. 'It's one of Gabriella's shoes.'

'Are you sure, Sir?' asked Sam.

'Yes. I'd know them anywhere. The Queen had them made especially for Miss Gabriella. So they went this way, but why? There is only that small village down here.'

'It's a port, Sir,' Sam reminded him. 'Sir Roland must have a boat waiting.'

'Yes, of course. Sam, if we're too late . . .' James could not finish for the awful thoughts which surfaced.

'I'll fetch the others, Sir. Please do not go ahead without me.'

James found he could not wait for Sam. He rode on ahead as fast as he could. The dawn was breaking on the mountains high above him so he could see his way more clearly. He hoped Gabriella would be able to delay Roland in some way. He wondered if Gabriella would be able to throw herself overboard if she were forced onto a boat. James knew she could swim but it had been many years since she had been able to do so. He wondered if she would have the strength to get to shore. He had to believe she would.

James rode into the village and found his way to a small quay. There was a carriage standing on the quay with its doors open but no sign of any persons inside. There was a large boat still moored to the quay. A few figures were hurrying to get it ready to sail. James could hear Sam and the others somewhere behind him but for the present he was on his own. James leaped off his horse, left it to its own devices, and jumped onto the boat as it was being cast off. He got rid of his coat in a hurry. He saw Roland coming towards him, looking angry.

Over the last few months James had spent most of his time helping the Queen with her new enterprise. So he had helped to clear out the warehouse and to install the heavy new stoves. He had wielded an axe to chop up logs to fuel them. The gardener had been spurred on to grow as much fruit as he could. So when spring arrived James had shovelled manure into a heavy wooden barrow and lugged it around to various fruit bushes to spread the contents around their roots. The bushes grew wonderfully. All of this activity had given James an appetite and consequently he had eaten large amounts of the Queen's good food. James was fit.

By contrast, Roland was lazy. He had driven Matilda around the town but had left the management of the horses to a stable lad. His only activity was to stroll to the library in the pursuit of Miss Valencie. Roland had eaten rich food washed down with large amounts of wine. He often felt queasy, but ignored the problem. On the morning after the ball when Roland had to face James, Roland had already drunk a large quantity of wine. There had been more waiting for him on the boat. Roland was none too steady on his feet.

It was a matter of a few seconds for James, whose anger lent him more strength, to dispatch Roland over the side of the boat. He nimbly got out of Roland's way as he lunged, tripped him up and pushed him the rest of the way over the side.

However, the other men on the boat were a different story. Two heavy seamen caught James between them and were about to throw him overboard to join Roland. This plan was thwarted when one of the men suddenly fell backwards in a faint. The other seaman let go in fright and tried to jump to land. He missed and fell in the sea. James was left to face a triumphant Gabriella who was holding a wooden pole in her hand. She dropped the pole and ran to James who caught her and hugged her to him tightly. He did not want to let go but Gabriella was trying to say something. Her face was buried tightly into James's coat.

'What, my love?' he asked, releasing her a little.

'The boat, James. It's about to go on those rocks.'

The opening to the port was small. This was perfect for harbouring craft in storms but not so good when trying to navigate the way out.

James spun around and saw she was right. 'Give me that pole, Gabriella. I'll push us off the rocks if I can. Can you try to adjust the tiller? Watch out for that sail.'

A small sail at the front of the boat had been raised to take the boat out of the harbour but it was sending them in the wrong direction.

'Which way is the wind blowing?' called Gabriella as she ran towards the stern.

'I don't know. Try moving the tiller to get us back to the quay. See what happens. I'll keep us off the rocks.'

The tiller was a cumbersome piece of apparatus which Gabriella found hard to move. She pushed it as hard as she could and slowly the boat responded. But the sail filled even more and sent them faster towards the other side of the harbour. James jumped to the other side of the boat and prepared himself for an inevitable crash. He didn't have time to get back to Gabriella to save her.

But Gabriella kept to her course. She held the tiller tightly by pushing with her feet up against one of the deck timbers. As the boat turned in the other direction the sail lost some of its puff and the boat just scraped past the harbour wall.

The boat was now headed for the quay so Gabriella let up on her hold of the tiller, which swung back to the centre.

'We are going to hit the quay, James,' cried Gabriella. 'Can you get that sail down?'

James looked up and saw that the sail was not pulling the boat as much as before. He decided it was better to use his time to fend the boat off the quay. 'Move us out the other way a bit, Gabriella. I'll be able to keep us off the wall.'

Gabriella pushed the tiller in the other direction a little and the boat missed the stone end of the pier. It scraped down the side of the quay at speed and crunched into the pebble beach. James fell against the bows and landed in a heap. Gabriella had hold of the tiller so broke her fall. They both heard a loud scream from inside the boat.

James picked himself up and waved to Sam who was anxiously watching from the quay. James saw that the guardsmen had captured two sodden figures and had tied them up back to back on the beach. One of the captured men was shouting and writhing about, trying to get free. The other man dug him in the ribs with his elbow and told him to stop pulling on the ropes because it was hurting him a lot. But James was more concerned about Gabriella. He hobbled to the stern where Gabriella was heading towards him. He caught her up as if never to let her go again. But his ankle gave way and they ended up in a pile on the decks.

'Steady, now,' laughed Gabriella.

'Are you hurt?' gasped James.

'Not at all, but it seems you are. We need to get off this boat. Stay where you are for a minute until I get one of the men to help us.'

'Gabriella, you have nothing on your feet,' said James.

'Yes, I know. I'll find something to put on in a minute.'

Gabriella got hold of a rope, tied it to the bows and threw it to one of the men on the beach. 'Make us safe, please,' she shouted. 'The boat could easily slide back into the harbour.'

Sam had run to the boat, so grabbed the end of the rope, took it to a nearby tree and tied it securely. He got one of his men to hoist him into the boat. 'Two of you come with me,' he shouted back to them as he ran to James.

'What was that scream we heard, Gabriella?' asked James.

'Oh no, I forgot Florence.'

'Florence? Whatever is she doing on this boat?'

'I'll tell you later. I'd better see if she is injured.' First she directed the two guardsmen to deal with the seaman lying on the deck, who was just recovering consciousness.

Sam was helping James to stand. 'We'll get you off, Sir, don't worry.'

'We'll wait for Gabriella. I'm not leaving this boat until she is safely on land. You might help her please.'

Gabriella came back with Florence clinging to her. Sam went to help and between them they got Florence to the bows where they could see men waiting on the beach.

'I can't get off this boat that way. I'll fall,' wailed Florence looking over the side. It was a long way down.

'We have to get off, Florence,' said Gabriella. 'Look, I'll go first and show you.' Gabriella leant over the side, swung her legs around and dropped into the arms of the men below.

'No, no,' cried Florence. 'I've hurt my leg. You can't make me do this.'

Sam beckoned to one of his men and they grabbed Florence, helped her over the side and gently lowered her down and then let go. She did not have far to fall and landed well, but it did not stop her from screaming.

Several people had now gathered to watch the spectacle and one of them kindly gave Gabriella a coat which she wrapped around Florence. A fisherman's wife offered to take the young lady home to give her some breakfast.

'That's very kind, thank you,' said Gabriella. 'But I think we will be leaving very soon. If I could trouble you to give this lady a hot drink it would be appreciated.'

'I'll fetch some hot milk, Miss,' said the woman.

Roland, who was tied to the other captive, called out to Gabriella. 'There has been a misunderstanding, Miss Valencie. Order this guard to release me.'

The guardsman told him to be quiet.

'Just wait until the King of Grelland hears what you have done to me,' threatened Roland.

The guardsman looked uncomfortable. 'I have my orders, Miss. I cannot release this man.'

'No,' said Gabriella. 'Under no circumstances are you to release this man. We'll see what our own King has to say about this matter. Check those ropes, if you please, and make sure they are fast.' With that Gabriella ignored Roland and turned back to the boat.

She watched as James was lifted off the boat and helped up the beach. Two fishermen said they would look after the boat if someone would tell them what was to be done with it. The Captain had a quick word with them before turning to James.

'We have three men in custody, Sir. What is best to do now, do you think?'

'Your men must need rest, Captain. Do you have any suggestions to make?'

'We'll manage, Sir, until we get back to the Guardhouse. Once these villains are locked up we can leave them in the care of other guardsmen until arrangements can be made to question them. We have two carriages at our disposal. You will need one, Sir, for yourself and the young ladies. I would like to leave Smithick and one other guardsman with you if that is agreeable.'

'Yes, thank you. The ladies will need rest before we travel any further. I believe there is an inn near the main road where we can rest for the day. Then, if Miss Gabriella is rested enough, I would like to travel back this evening. We will keep the Palace's carriage. Whose is the other one?'

'I believe it was hired by Sir Roland to bring his party to the ball, Sir.'

'So Roland's wife must have stayed at the Palace last night. What I suggest is that you use that carriage to take the arrested men back to the city. Then, once the horses have been rested, Roland's wife can use it to travel back to the inn, where she can collect her sister on her way home. We can safely leave Miss Florence at that inn while she waits.' James had no desire to travel back to the Palace with Florence in the carriage. 'I know you will keep those men securely guarded. Under no circumstances is Roland to talk his way out of being put in prison until we can find out exactly what happened.'

'Of course, Sir.' The Captain issued orders for the men to be loaded into the hired carriage. A fisherman's wife brought out blankets for the men who had got wet. The Captain thanked her and promised to return them in due course.

Roland struggled and shouted at James but James was too tired to respond. The guardsmen quickly threw a blanket over Roland's head to keep him quiet and bundled him into the carriage.

Gabriella helped Florence get into the Palace's carriage and climbed in behind her. Sam made sure James managed to get in too, and then went to catch the bridles of the horses to turn the equipment around. He climbed onto the driving seat with the other guardsman and they slowly left the village.

The small crowd stayed talking on the quay for the rest of the morning. A surprise visit by the Prince to their quiet village was not something they would forget in a long time.

The three passengers in the carriage sank back into their seats. Florence grumbled that her leg hurt.

'It's best you do not say anything at present, Florence,' said Gabriella. 'We can discuss what you have done after you have had some sleep at the inn. I cannot concentrate on your troubles at the moment.'

Florence lapsed into a moody silence but laid her head against the seat and soon closed her eyes.

James and Gabriella whispered to each other on the other side of the carriage. 'Is your ankle hurting again, James?' asked Gabriella.

'Not as bad as last time, thanks. It's just a bruise I think. But you must be tired.'

'Yes, but very happy, thanks to you.'

A little further down the road James recovered enough to notice that Gabriella still did not have anything on her feet, but she had one shoe in her hand. James took something out of his pocket. He pulled out a handkerchief and dusted the object.

'I think this may be yours,' said James, presenting Gabriella with her other shoe.

Chapter Thirty Three

As they travelled back that evening, James was content simply to have Gabriella safely beside him. Neither of them was inclined to talk about the events of the night. James held Gabriella's hand while they watched the sun go down from the carriage window. The relief James felt after the horror of what could have happened left him tired. He knew they would talk once the shock had worn off.

Now that Gabriella was secure and she no longer had to fight for her own safety or that of James, she felt all the anxiety leave her slowly. She knew eventually she would have to explain what had happened but for the present she wanted to enjoy being in safe hands. She hoped in time to forget everything that had taken place. She would face recounting Roland's treachery in a few days' time when she had recovered.

They arrived at Gabriella's home to find Nanny waiting for them on the doorstep. There were tears in her eyes. Gabriella got out of the carriage to be wrapped up in Nanny's arms.

'The Captain of the Guard told us a little of what had happened,' said Nanny. 'We knew you were safe but it didn't stop me worrying. Come away in now and have something to eat. Will Prince James come in with you?'

'No, Nanny, he must let the Queen see he is still alive. She is as worried as you, I expect.'

James had got out of the carriage to deliver Gabriella to

the door, but he turned now, waved to them both and got back in. 'I'll visit tomorrow morning, if I may.'

Gabriella waved until the carriage was out of sight. Nanny led her charge into a warm kitchen where a large quantity of food awaited them. 'I had to do something, Gabriella,' said Nanny, by way of explanation.

Gabriella smiled. 'I only need a little, Nanny, thank you. I need rest more. I can eat tomorrow.'

So Nanny soon had Gabriella tucked up in a feather bed. She stayed until Gabriella was fast asleep.

James met a similar reception at the Palace. The Queen had been relieved by the Captain's report but was happier once James was home. The King shook James's hand in delight to see him safe. Mr. Secretary hovered in the background but said how pleased he was to see the Prince. Jenny and Nell had put flowers in James's room and had done everything they could think of to make his return comfortable.

The occupants of the Palace slept well that night.

* * *

Two days later Gabriella and the Prince were asked to attend the King. The Queen had placed a tray of tea and biscuits in the library to make the couple feel more relaxed.

The King apologised for the necessity of asking them what had happened. 'We need to know in order to decide what to do with Roland.'

'Yes, of course, Sir,' said James. 'You know most of what happened to me, but I believe Gabriella's story will be of more importance.'

'Well then, if you feel able to tell us it would help considerably, Gabriella,' said the King.

'I had to piece it together from what Florence told me,' said Gabriella. 'It seems her mother had not told her the story of her gaming debts, so Florence thought I had cheated her out of her inheritance. In this frame of mind she agreed to help Roland with his plan to capture me. He did not tell her the truth, of course. It appears he told Florence he would get her inheritance back, but first he had to bring me back to Grelland in order to speak to a judge at the Court in Derville where my actions would be looked into. Then Florence was sure to get back what was rightfully hers.'

'Did she believe this fantastic story?' asked the King.

'It seems she did. Roland even told her that an appointment had been made at the Court for the day after the ball. So it was imperative, from Florence's point of view, to make sure I attended. Roland said I would never come if I was told where I was going, so he had to ask Florence to assist in a little deception. He said I would not be hurt and it would simply make matters happen more quickly than if they had to ask lawyers to force me to attend the court. He said I would be glad, in the end, to get everything over and done with.'

'So Florence went along with this plan in order to get more money?'

'Yes, she did. She told me that Matilda was content with what she was now receiving but Florence did not believe it was enough for her. Matilda had a home of her own and now had enough money to manage it. Matilda thought Roland would also provide money eventually, so she was willing to wait. I believe Matilda did have some notion that her mother had been involved in gaming. According to Florence, Matilda has imposed a strict budget in the household. She gives her mother board and lodging and very little else.'

'So if Matilda is grateful for what your father left her, why is Florence not so?' pursued the King.

'Florence believed her mother's story. She had been brought up to believe there was a lot of money waiting for them when my father died. Florence knew nothing about her mother's card parties. I suspect Matilda knew all along.'

'I suppose we will never understand the motives in that

girl's head,' said the King. 'But how did she get you into that carriage?'

'Florence sent one of the hired maids to tell me she was feeling ill. The maid told me Florence was outside the front door thinking that fresh air would help. When I got there the maid said that Florence must have ordered a carriage to take her to her lodgings in order to rest. So I got into the carriage to see how ill she was. The door slammed and locked behind me and within a few seconds we were moving.'

James took Gabriella's cup and filled it with more tea. 'It's all over now,' he said gently. 'You might just tell the King about leaving your shoe at the turning.'

'Another childhood game,' said Gabriella smiling. 'If, for instance, Peter got abducted by pirates or highwaymen, he only left signs of where he had been taken on paths that deviated from the main one. If he were taken along a main road there was no need to leave a sign, but a side road needed to be marked. If I remember rightly he never got taken too far by our imaginary kidnapper before he let himself be found by James and me. We had the sandwiches, after all.'

The King smiled at such antics. 'It seems to have stood you in good stead. But how did you know where you were?'

'It was not easy because it was dark, but the road to Grelland is quite straight. We took that turning to the port at speed and Florence fell off the seat. I believed it had to be a turning off the main road, so while Florence was engaged in sorting herself out, I managed to throw my shoe out of the window.'

'I still do not understand why Roland was taking you to sea. Where were you going?'

'I do not know. We were both thrown into a small cabin and someone locked that door too. It took me a while to get it open. Florence was as surprised as I was.'

'How did you get the door unlocked? Those cabin doors are usually quite strong.'

'I locked myself in my own bedroom once and could not get the door open. Mr. Georges put a piece of paper under the door and told me to put the key on it. He dragged the piece of paper back with the key on it and unlocked the door from the other side. So I did the same with the cabin door. There was a good space under the door and the key had been left in the lock. There was a sheet on the couch in the cabin, so I pushed it under the door and used a hairpin to push the key out. It took some time which is why I was late to help James. Have you been able to find out why I was put on a boat, Sir?' Gabriella asked the King.

'Not yet, but we will institute some enquiries. We have enough information to hold Roland and to send a letter to the King of Grelland for his suggestions and his opinion of what is best to do. We do not want to take any action before that so as not to upset anyone. But I believe Grelland's King will be reasonable.'

Chapter Thirty Four

The month of August was warm and sunny. Nanny and Gabriella picked berries and used them to teach some of the Queen's new staff how to make jam. The Queen did not want Gabriella to spend much time doing this because there were preparations to be made for the wedding.

James and Gabriella had decided to have a quiet wedding. They had had enough excitement for a long time. They knew the whole country would want to celebrate so the Queen suggested that after the ceremony they have a garden party for the local townspeople. The King was to think about what else could be done and he would consult with the couple before making any arrangements. The wedding was set for the beginning of September when, all being well, the sun would shine and before any winter cold set in.

Gabriella had little to do to get her wedding clothes ready because her mother had carefully packed her own clothes, waiting for when Gabriella would need them. They were packed with lavender cushions and Nanny had replaced these each year. All they had to do was to take the clothes out of the wrappings and air them in the sunshine.

There were gloves, slippers, petticoats and all manner of small items. The design of the wedding dress itself was simple but it was made of the most expensive silk. There was a shawl of the same material should the day be a little chilly. The cuffs and collar of the dress were embroidered in complicated patterns and trimmed with lace. A delicate lace train flowed beautifully from the shoulders. The ensemble set off Gabriella's dark hair wonderfully.

Nanny had declined to be a matron of honour. She said weddings were for young people. She would be proud to sit at the front, if that was permissible.

'I could not allow you to sit anywhere else, Nanny. You will take my mother's place, which is what you have been doing for a long time. Mr. Georges has kindly said he will give me away, although I don't want to be given away and I hope you will stay with me forever.'

'In that case, dear, I would like to ask if Mr. Georges and I can live near you in the cottage at the Palace. This house has been good to live in, but there are some bad memories as well as good. It's too big for just the two of us, anyway. We looked at the cottage and it would suit us well, if you are sure it is acceptable for us to go there.'

'That is the best news ever, Nanny. You will be near me, which will make me feel much more comfortable, especially at first. You must take whatever furniture you want from here. It leaves me without a bridesmaid, though. Do you think Miss Jemima would accompany me?' asked Gabriella, her happiness overflowing into merriment. 'I don't think it would be good to ask Peter if he would be a page boy.'

So Gabriella and Nanny made their plans, with their future being brighter than either could have hoped.

* * *

Towards the end of August the King was able to give James and Gabriella some more information concerning Roland. The King and Mr. Secretary sat with them in the library with the sun pouring in through the long windows.

'First of all, there was no appointment made at the Court in Derville. That was a pure fabrication on Roland's part, which I am sure you knew already. Nothing was found to be wrong with your father's will, that is, the first one. The second one was proved to be a fraud. We asked our own judge to confirm your solicitor's findings and the judge was convinced, when he compared the signatures and other matters, that the second one was a forgery. He accepted that Mr. Browning had acted properly in the matter of your inheritance, Gabriella. Mrs. Sertus's actions were condemned and her exile approved. All of that is what you expected, of course.'

'Yes, thank you,' said Gabriella. 'It is a relief to get it all settled finally.'

'Roland's affairs are still causing us some problems but we believe we have discovered most of what he intended to do. He had instituted proceedings to have his marriage to Matilda annulled. She got the papers the day after returning from the ball. She contested them, of course, and she won that quarrel. Roland's criminal activities tarnished his reputation, so he did not get a sympathetic hearing. His motives for the marriage were to defraud James out of his position as heir to the throne, so the fact that Matilda concealed her real name was not considered to be a reason for the marriage to be annulled. Roland now is obliged to provide for Matilda.'

'So will she stay in Grelland?' asked Gabriella.

'Yes. Roland has been convicted of treason and is to be exiled to one of the more remote islands off Grelland's shores. Matilda is entitled to Roland's house and estate. If she is astute in managing them, along with her allowance from your father, she should have a reasonable income.'

'I am pleased, Sir,' said Gabriella. 'I was treated badly by my supposed step-mother and Matilda was influenced by her, but I believe Matilda has not sided with her mother in the matter of the will and has accepted that the fault lay with her mother and not me.'

'There is some room for optimism that Matilda will turn

out well. She had a bad example in her mother but you must remember that she also had your good example to follow. She has seen the dire outcome of gaming and has taken steps to avoid any future possibility that her mother will incur debts again. Matilda made mistakes and while her mother lives, she will not have an easy life, but it could be worse.'

'She should be very comfortable once she has sorted out that estate and the house. Florence complained that Roland's house was very run down,' said Gabriella. 'But from the little I was told I believe it will be possible to make some rooms comfortable without much outlay. Matilda was not given much money while her mother had the reins of my house, so she will know how to manage economically.'

'That has answered some of our questions, Sir,' said James. 'But where was Roland taking Gabriella on that boat and what had he planned to do with her?'

'This is not easy for me to tell you, James. Roland was going to hide Gabriella on one of the many islands off the coast of Grelland. He believed the annulment of his marriage would not take very long and he planned to force Gabriella to marry him immediately on his release from Matilda.'

James went cold with anger. 'Just let me get my hands on him,' he said, getting up from his chair.

'No, dear boy, you can't take matters into your own hands, despite the provocation,' said the King.

Gabriella had also got up from her chair and was standing between James and the door. 'James, I cannot cope with you being at risk of harm anymore. Please allow the King to deal with Roland. Remember you threw Roland in the sea, which was very degrading for him. He must have got very cold and I expect he was wishing then that he had not tried to capture me.'

James calmed down a little. 'Maybe so, but it was not a just punishment for him.'

'No, but just think. Roland must have thought he was going to drown. If that other seaman had not got hold of him and dragged him to the shore, he probably would have done. Just imagine how humiliated Roland must have been sitting on that beach tied up, dripping wet with seawater. I expect he was covered in seaweed too.' Gabriella laughed at the thought and elicited a brief grin from James.

'Maybe so,' said James reluctantly. 'But why did Roland want to be heir to the throne anyway?'

'Ah, yes, that is quite interesting,' said the King. 'When Roland was delivered to the guardhouse, there was little space for him so he was placed in a room with a pickpocket. The young lad was soon released with a warning but was arrested again a few days later. The lad had taken something out of Roland's pocket and had tried to sell it. He made the mistake of taking it to a small shop in a back street, thinking the shop-owner more likely to be open to shady dealings. The shop-owner was one of our most honourable merchants. He caught the lad and sent his assistant for the Guard. The lad was trying to sell a small lump of gold.'

'And this was the thing he had taken out of Roland's pocket?' asked James.

'That's correct. We got letters from the King of Grelland apologising for Roland's behaviour. The King had been warned by his advisers of possible action by Roland in an attempt to get the gold for himself. Unfortunately the King did not believe there was a real threat. But, by way of compensation, he has offered to send two of the country's professors to find the exact place the gold was found. We sent our own College people to accompany them and should have the results soon.'

'Will that take long? They must have a wide area to search,' said James.

'Not too wide. We deduced that the gold must be on land which belongs to the Crown, in other words to you and me, James. The gold was probably found on land close to Grelland's border too. But don't get your hopes up because although gold can be found here it is often only a small amount in one place.'

'Gabriella,' asked James, 'are you thinking as I am?'

'Yes, I think so. We would like to help in the search, Sir.'

'I do not believe I can allow you to do that. It is rough work and not the place for our future Princess.'

'We were raised with a freedom we enjoyed, Sir,' said James. 'I do not think we will be able to alter out ways to be the sort of people who sit around at court all day. I do not believe you would want us to do so either.'

'There is something in that, James, I agree,' said the King thoughtfully. 'But still, is this the sort of work you want to get involved in?'

'Most certainly, sir,' said James. 'It's our future, don't forget. If we find the gold there is a chance I might be able to support Gabriella instead of the other way round. There is another matter too which must not be overlooked. We know the land around here better than most people and certainly more so than the professors from Grelland.'

'And,' added Gabriella, 'if there had been any disturbance to the land when Roland tried to find the gold we would know. The professors might overlook something if it were small which we would not.'

'Oh, very well, then. But do not think you will always get your own way when you both live under my roof,' said the King severely, knowing full well that he would always give them what they wanted if he could. 'Take that young guardsman with you, what's his name?'

'Sam,' said James. He thanked the King, who was pleased to see James returning to his normal good humour. Gabriella and James left the library while making plans to meet later. 'Wear some old clothes, Gabriella.'

'I have plenty of those, at least. Nanny will make some sandwiches,' said Gabriella with a chuckle.

'Just like old times,' said James happily.

Chapter Thirty Five

Susie stared critically at her mistress. 'Excuse me, Miss, but surely you are not visiting with the Prince in those old clothes. Will I fetch one of your prettier dresses?'

'No, thank you, Susie. Today the Prince and I have to look for something and I do not want to get my good clothes dirty.'

'I'm good at finding things, Miss,' said Susie casually. She was making some toast for Gabriella while Nanny busied herself with packing a lunch basket.

'If you are going to look for something you need lots of help,' said Bob, who had devoured his breakfast and was bringing in an armful of logs for Nanny's cooking stove. Both Bob and Susie looked wistfully at Gabriella.

'Do you need them today, Nanny?' asked Gabriella.

'Not at all. I'd be glad of a quiet day if they could help you. I'd have to put in some more food but it won't take me long.'

'Oh, very well then,' said Gabriella with a smile. 'Go and get ready and do not be too long.'

'I'm ready,' said Bob. 'I can carry the food.'

'I only have to change my shoes, Miss, if you could wait for me, please,' said Susie anxiously.

When James arrived with the carriage he found Gabriella's party waiting for him. 'Reinforcements, I see,' said James. 'I have some of my own. Two of Sam's friends begged for the privilege of helping their future Queen.' Two guardsmen sheepishly bowed to Gabriella and tried to take the basket from Bob. There was a tussle but Bob won and said he would take care of it and ride standing on the backboard of the carriage with the basket at his feet.

They set off down the road while James explained to Gabriella the progress which had been made so far.

'The professors from Grelland got their men to search for gold in the rivers and streams. A few yielded some good results. So we are to search in the hills above some of these spots. Others are looking too in different areas. The professors said the rain washes the gold down the hills into the streams so we only have to look on the surface for the seams. They have given me a sample to give us an idea of what to find.' He gave the small chunk of metal to Gabriella. 'We'll have to scrape the surface but we do not have to dig, which is a good thing. But there should be evidence of Roland's searches so it might not be difficult.'

Susie stared at the gold sample. 'Oh, Miss, I've never seen anything like this before. We'll find it for you, no trouble.'

'I'm sure we will, Susie.'

Sam stopped the carriage at the end of a track in a clearing. Everyone got out. The horses were unhitched and allowed to graze in a nearby meadow. James sent two of the guardsmen with Bob in one direction with instructions of what to look for. He kept Sam and Susie with him and Gabriella. 'Back here for lunch,' he told the others.

They set off happily and spread themselves out over the hillside. Susie rushed backwards and forwards with stones for the Prince to look at but she soon slowed down as the heat of the day increased.

At lunch time James took the whole party to the river bank. Bob said he was sure it was nearer to dinner time than lunch, and he was sorry he had not found the gold for the Prince just yet, but he was certain he would find it before too long.

The afternoon progressed quickly but there were no

results that day. The following days took on a similar routine. Their initial enthusiasm slowed and they took longer lunch breaks, with James and Gabriella wandering away from the rest of the party to paddle in the streams or look at a view.

'It doesn't matter that we have not found anything, James,' said Gabriella one afternoon. 'We have had a lovely time. I believe Susie and Bob will be loyal to us for the rest of their lives.'

'Which is a good thing, since they are to help at the Palace from now on. I'm glad to get to know them a little better.'

It was not until the tenth day that they found the gold. Late one afternoon, Bob had tumbled down a ravine and Sam had jumped after him to pull him out. They both landed in the stream but as they climbed out Sam noticed some ground which had been disturbed. There was jubilation when Sam picked up a small piece of rough yellow metal.

They all returned home delighted but tired, with James giving the guardsmen strict instructions to mention it to no-one until the area could be secured. James took Gabriella home, promising to take her to visit the professors on the next day.

'I'm glad we have found the gold, James, but I'm pleased we did not find it any sooner,' said Gabriella. 'These last few days have been heavenly for me, after all the trouble of the past two years. Thank you, dear friend.'

Chapter Thirty Six

In due course the gold was extracted from the ground. The seam did indeed run out before much had been mined, but gold fever had run riot and there were discoveries of small seams in other areas. Together the gold amounted to a reasonable amount of income for the country and the King set about using it wisely.

The King got many requests. The Queen wanted larger premises for her jam making industry; James had endorsed the local college's request for funding for education; the townspeople asked for better flood defences. They also asked for a new roof for the town hall, a park to take walks in of a Sunday and a new road-sweeper to replace the old man who no longer did an adequate job.

The King called a halt to any further requests, saying that what he did for the local town he would have to do for all the others. He agreed with the need for flood defences but reminded them that his immediate priority was to arrange a wedding.

The townspeople forgot their grievances and instead threw their energies into the coming nuptials. The Palace received a steady stream of well-wishers presenting their gifts for the happy couple. Mr. Secretary wrote down their names in a book. Even the little girl who brought an apple had her name written in fine script. She stared at it in awe.

The Queen mentioned this to Gabriella and James at a

small dinner she had cooked for them. 'It's very touching to see the kindness of our subjects,' she commented.

'Yes, but it has given us a dilemma,' said James.

'In what way, dear?' asked the Queen.

'We did not realise our affairs would be of such interest. We thought we could get married quietly without fuss. It's what Gabriella has asked for and I would like to give her what she wants. But I wonder now if we might do something to include the local people in the celebrations afterwards.'

'Thank you, dear James,' said Gabriella fondly. 'But if our wedding should be public, then so be it. I think I will enjoy it after all. And I cannot disappoint everyone.'

'That would present difficulties of its own,' said the King. 'We cannot fit everyone into the chapel you have chosen to marry in. The townspeople will understand that you wish to make some gesture towards your parents' memory, Gabriella. They will respect that, but perhaps we could have a procession from the chapel to the Palace which could include everyone who wishes.'

'The garden party we decided upon could be arranged for a larger number, if you agree,' suggested the Queen. 'It's unlikely to rain and with all the donations we have food enough for several towns.'

So in a flurry of activity the wedding preparations came to fulfilment. When the rest of the country realised the people living close to the Palace were to be included in the celebrations, they requested that the Prince and his bride visit them, if they would be kind enough to take a tour of every town in Essenia.

The King thought it would be too taxing for the newly-weds but James and Gabriella said they would love to take such a tour. In an attempt to suit everyone, Mr. Secretary arranged for a quiet day for the newly-weds between the visits to each principle town, to take into consideration the King's request that the couple did not overly exert themselves.

Mr. Secretary sent letters to each town hall stating the day the Prince and Princess were to arrive and strict instructions to the townspeople to allow the couple to have time to themselves afterwards. The letter suggested that each town make a list of places the Prince and his bride may like to see, to acquaint them with the beauty of the country they would one day rule.

It was decided that Nanny, Mr. Georges, Susie and Bob would move into their new places in the Palace while the tour took place.

So it was with joy that Gabriella and James married in the chapel. They were accompanied by Peter and Jemima. As a gift, Gabriella presented them with the deeds to her old home, and the delight on their faces was reward enough. Peter was too overcome for words and a few tears of happiness fell down Jemima's cheeks. Jemima's brother, who had also travelled to the wedding, shook Gabriella's hand and said he would be forever in her debt.

The ceremony was not marred by any quarrels or disputes over names but was conducted with dignity. Nanny had to dab her eyes with her handkerchief, of course, but was comforted by the Queen. Gabriella looked radiant and after James had kissed her, he told her it was the happiest moment of his life.

Immediately afterwards, Gabriella and James had a few private minutes to lay Gabriella's flowers on the graves of her parents. After this solemn act and a few tears from Gabriella, James and his bride turned to receive the cheers of the crowd.

They joined the procession to the Palace secure in the knowledge that, after all their adventures, little could mar their quiet happiness in the future.

About the Author

Author Bridget Cantwell wrote her first book 'Loose Chippings' after finding herself living in a shed with no water or electricity. Humour was the key to her survival. Bridget lives in the West of Ireland. She has a much-loved daughter, a scientist, the source of a lot of unusual information.

Printed in the United States
By Bookmasters